WORD PERFECT

LIZ HARRIS

HEYWOOD PRESS

1

———

L os Angeles, California
July, in the late 1960s

LEIGH PULLED open the floor-to-ceiling glass doors, stepped out on to the decking and gazed around her at the profusion of flowers that flanked the veranda, and at the deep green sweep of the garden, beyond which lay a band of sparkling blue.

She took a few steps forward and stood still, drinking in the beauty of the scene. As the musky fragrance of the warm Californian evening wrapped itself around her, she felt herself completely relax for the first time that day.

Her past twelve hours had been truly amazing, and had fled by in a haze of excitement.

She, Leigh Carter from London, was going to be working for one of the best-known Hollywood actors for a couple of weeks, maybe even longer, and living in absolute luxury while she did so. If it wasn't completely mad of her, she'd have pinched herself to make sure she wasn't dreaming!

From the moment the wrought-iron gates at the entrance to Matt Hunter's drive had opened, allowing her to drive up to the imposing low white house, to the moment just now when she'd risen from the table having had her evening meal with Tom Grover, the secretary she'd be temporarily replacing, and Van Attwood, Matt Hunter's PA—a meal that had been made and served by the resident cook—it was as if she'd stepped into another world.

Matt Hunter was in pre-production work for his forth-coming film, and wouldn't be back till the following day, she'd been told on arrival, so she'd been interviewed by Tom and Van.

They'd offered her the job on the spot, and she'd then been introduced to Conchita, the cook and housekeeper, and Conchita's husband, Armando, Matt Hunter's driver. Conchita and Armando lived, she was told, above the white garage block that lay on the far side of the drive.

After that, Tom had shown her around the office she'd be using, and then had handed her over to Van to fill her in on everything else.

She'd had a quick sandwich lunch, at which she'd been unable to eat very much, and then Van had shown her around the house, taking her along corridors that were lined with signed photographs of Matt Hunter's well-known actor friends, and through the large den, the dining room, the theatre room, the wing where her new boss slept, the wing where Van had a suite, and finally to the suite that would temporarily be hers.

She'd fallen in love with the house, and the open air feeling everywhere, caused in part by the large glass doors that ran along the back of the house, opening out on to the veranda.

They'd finished their tour at the indoor pool and gym at the far end of the house, and then she'd driven back to her Brentwood apartment to collect sufficient clothes and personal items to last her a couple of weeks. She'd be given a place for her car in the garage block, Van had told her before she left, and also a remote control to open the gates for whenever she wanted to drive herself anywhere.

After she'd returned with her clothes and had unpacked, she'd eaten in the den with Tom and Van— enchiladas stuffed with refried beans, onion and red peppers, accompanied by a glass of white wine before the meal and one with it.

Then she'd wandered out on to the veranda to catch the last rays of the sun as it sank into the tree-lined horizon, casting dark purple shadows that stealthily lengthened across the grass.

She looked happily around her.

In all of the months she'd been temping in Los Angeles, and in the year before that when she'd lived in San Francisco, she'd never been in a house that came remotely close in its design, and in its sense of comfort and luxury, to this, and she intended to savour every single minute of what was bound to be a once-in-a-lifetime experience.

There was a slight movement of air, and she glanced to her right. Van Attwood had come out on to the veranda and was standing next to her.

'Lovely, isn't it?' he said, his gaze on the garden. 'Whatever the time of day.'

'It's really magical. I still can't believe I'm actually going to be living here for a while.'

'I can understand that,' he said with a smile. 'I don't

know about you,' he went on after a slight pause, 'but I like a short walk round the garden after my evening meal. Would you care to join me?'

Not really, she thought. She was far too tired.

The moment she'd started to relax, she'd realised how shattered she was after the excitement of getting the job and then everything else that had followed. All she now wanted to do was get some sleep.

She opened her mouth to say that she was ready to turn in, and then hesitated.

She might come across as unfriendly and ungrateful if she refused to accompany Van on his walk, and she wouldn't want that.

After all, he'd approved her for the position, had taken the trouble to show her around, and had done all he could to fill her in about the job, trying to anticipate what she'd need to know as he recognised that she was being thrown in at the deep end, having to start work the following morning.

So reluctantly, she agreed.

With the light fast fading, they started to stroll along one of the paved paths leading away from the house and into the spotlit garden. Ahead of them lay the large illuminated pool, a vivid greenish-blue in a paved surround that was flanked with lavender bushes. Beyond the pool stood a low white house.

'That's the cabana,' Van told her. 'We'll take a quick look at it and then call it a day. When you've seen the cabana, you'll have seen just about everything there is to see.'

She stared wearily at the cabana. It wasn't that far away, but it was still too far to go at the end of a very long day, she thought, and she'd seen more than enough for one day.

'Don't you think we ought to be getting back?' she ventured. 'It's quite dark now.'

'Not a bit of it. The night's still young.' Van gave Leigh's elbow a friendly squeeze.

With a deep-down sigh, she followed him on to the poolside patio, trying to keep her mind on what he was saying, and not on her longing for sleep. He obviously wanted to make sure that she understood the areas of her responsibility and of his.

He looked after the data management, he told her, and helped Matt Hunter with various aspects of his business affairs, and he made Matt's travel arrangements, including getting any visas he needed and his accommodation.

Also, he was the person who would meet and greet any visitors to the house. In addition, he looked after Matt's diary, although obviously in conjunction with Tom, and both he and Tom could make appointments.

'That sounds quite a lot,' she murmured when he paused for breath.

He inclined his head in acknowledgement.

As secretary, he continued, her responsibility would be to screen Matt Hunter's phone calls and take care of his correspondence as was appropriate. She would be expected to take notes at the meetings he went to, take dictation as per his request, and generally correspond on his behalf.

He was still in full flow when they reached the cabana, by then describing with enthusiasm the parties that Matt would occasionally throw for his friends, some of which were held in the cabana, which was equipped with showers and changing rooms, a sun lounge, a well-stocked bar and a games area that included a pool table.

'And, of course, a couple of bedrooms,' he added, arching a thin smile in her direction.

In a trice, a sudden bolt of alarm ran through her, driving out every vestige of tiredness.

She hoped to goodness she hadn't made a really bad mistake in agreeing to go for a walk with Van when darkness was already starting to set in! After all, when it came to it, she hardly knew the man. Biting her lower lip, she glanced at him.

He turned towards her at that very moment, and smiled pleasantly.

She shook herself. She was being silly, letting her imagination run away with her.

Van was just going out of his way to be kind, which was what he'd been doing since first thing that morning.

As soon as the agency, which Van had used frequently and trusted implicitly, had received his urgent request the day before for immediate temporary secretarial help, they'd sent Leigh's details to Van, Tom and Matt Hunter, saying that she came with the highest of recommendations.

Van had promptly phoned her to come in for an interview first thing that morning. The agency told Leigh they'd send another temp to the company for which she'd been working, and she'd driven straight to Matt Hunter's house.

Since her arrival, Van had gone out of his way to try to make her feel at home, which was especially important as she'd be living in the house. He'd been only too aware of the short amount of time before Tom had to leave. With Tom's mother extremely ill, he was desperate to fly to Chicago at the earliest possible opportunity.

In her gratitude for his kindness to her, she'd laughed at his unfunny jokes, agreed with his every remark, and soon they'd seemed to be getting on as easily as old friends.

But they weren't old friends.

They'd known each other for a few hours only.

In spite of the warmth of the evening, she felt suddenly cold.

If only she hadn't been so desperate to get the job!

Working for an actor was the dream job of every Hollywood secretary. It was going to be an amazing opportunity, and she'd been frantic not to lose it. And the money would be very useful.

The agency had told her that the job paid above the normal rate, and because they appreciated that she'd have to start immediately and live in, and therefore cancel any plans she might have made, they were going to pay her more than she usually earned.

The extra money couldn't be coming at a better time.

Four years earlier, clutching her Resident Alien Card, she'd arrived in San Francisco, a place she'd long wanted to visit, where she was to look after two children for a year. The family for which she'd be working had paid for her flight, and were going to deduct the cost of the ticket from her salary.

She'd intended to stay on in California for a further two years after her year with the family was up, travelling around a bit, making some money and saving some of it, and would then return to England.

At first things had gone as planned. She'd saved a large part of what she'd earned in her year in San Francisco, and had then travelled down to Los Angeles, where she'd had no trouble at all in finding work as an agency temp.

Her time in LA had been so fantastic that she'd stayed on for a third year, working throughout her time there for the same agency as they'd sent her to a variety of such interesting jobs. And her social life, too, had been terrific.

It was her savings that had let her down.

She'd managed to save a little, but not as much as she'd have liked. As fast as she saved it, she seemed to spend it!

But she had only herself to blame.

She'd thrown herself with wild abandon into life in California.

She'd bought clothes in ultra-hip boutiques, eaten more meals in Scandia and Lawry's than she could count, been to just about every nightclub and piano bar in LA, taken riding lessons and then ridden in the Hollywood Hills on many a morning, and she'd gone frequently to Palm Springs and Las Vegas, losing money whenever she went there.

She'd had fun, fun, fun!

But the flip side was that she had nowhere near the amount she'd counted on taking back to England with her.

And she really did have to go back before too long. She knew deep down that it was time she got a proper job.

If she carried on doing what she'd been doing for very much longer, she'd become so used to work of an undemanding nature that she'd lose the confidence to apply for anything more challenging, which could offer her real long-term satisfaction.

And she knew herself well enough to know that in the fullness of time, she'd come to regret allowing herself to become institutionalised as it were, like a life-serving prisoner.

It was already happening, she could tell, and anxious to stop the rot from spreading, she'd been intending to return to England in September or October.

Of course, that proper job didn't absolutely have to be in England—it could be in the States. She was thoroughly enjoying living there, and it wouldn't be any hardship to stay there forever.

But it would be a huge step to leave England once and for all, and she wasn't certain she wanted to do that.

The only way to find out where she really wanted to settle, she'd decided, was to go back to England and try living there for a few months. Her Resident Alien Card allowed her to stay in the States for as long as she wanted, provided she didn't stay out of the US for more than a year, so she had up to a year in England in which to decide whether she wanted to live there or in California.

So going back was a must, and for that she needed some money.

If she didn't have a little more than she now had, she'd struggle to support herself in the first few weeks she was back in London, and she might well be forced to do the very thing she didn't want to do—move back in with her parents.

They'd never been really close, and she strongly suspected that they'd be no keener on the idea of her living with them than she was to live with them, so it would be an unhappy experience for them all, and one that would weight the scales in favour of Los Angeles, which wouldn't really be giving England a fair chance.

So the opportunity to work for Matt Hunter couldn't have come at a better time. And having got the job, she'd been determined to keep it.

That had been hovering in her mind all day.

But looking back, she could now see all too clearly that in her enthusiasm to ensure that Van liked her and would want to give her the help she was certain to need in the following few days, she might have overdone it and unwittingly sent out the wrong signals.

And in retrospect, having a glass of wine before dinner when she'd hardly eaten a thing in the day, and then another with her meal, hadn't been the wisest thing to do.

She most certainly hadn't been thinking clearly when she'd gone along with Van's suggestion of joining him for his nightly walk.

But her head was crystal clear now. And she was acutely aware that she was alone with a man she hardly knew.

A tremor of cold fear shot through her.

'Here we are.' Van Attwood's voice cut through her thoughts.

The solid wood door of the cabana faced her.

She took a step back as Van inserted the key into the lock, but he put his hand gently, but firmly, under her elbow and ushered her into the darkness within. The door clicked shut behind them.

She stood still, her back to the door, her heart beating unevenly. Van flicked a switch on the wall and subtle lighting filled the room, removing the sense of threat. Releasing her elbow, he went across to a long mahogany bar on the far side of the room.

She knew she could easily turn round and leave, but everything looked so much more normal in the light and she didn't feel quite as anxious as she had a few minutes earlier.

What's more, if she ran out, Van would guess at once the sort of person she thought he was. And if she was wrong, she might have seriously offended him, and possibly even lost the precious job, for no reason at all.

But suppose her earlier instinct, and her alarm, had been right?

What should she do, she agonised.

She looked across at Van. He was filling two glasses from a bottle of red wine.

'Perhaps it's a bit too late for work now,' she said, trying to keep her voice from shaking.

'I agree.' He picked up the glasses and came towards her, a smile on his lips, his steel-grey eyes glittering in the reflected light. 'So we're not going to work—we're going to relax. You'll like this wine—it's a good vintage.' He held out a glass.

She stared at the glass

In a moment of wild hope, she thought she heard the sound of footsteps in the garden. She listened hard. But no, all was silent. Her heart sank—she must've been mistaken.

She shook her head. 'Thanks, Van, but I really don't want anything else to drink. To be honest, I'm shattered, and I'd like to go back to my room now.'

She heard the sound again, and it was closer this time. There *was* someone there. Relief swept through her.

She saw Van glance swiftly towards the door.

Then he moved smoothly across to the long coffee table in front of the L-shaped sofa, bent down and placed the glasses on the table.

He straightened up. 'You must forgive me, Leigh,' he said, his voice full of apology as he came back to her. 'I've been real thoughtless. Of course you're tired—you've had a long day. You shouldn't have had to remind me. Come on, we'll go back now.'

Before she could move, she heard the cabana door swing open.

'And what exactly is going on?'

At the sound of a man's voice behind her, a voice ice-cold with anger, she and Van spun round and faced the door.

A tall man with broad shoulders stood framed in the doorway. The line of his jaw was hard and angular, and his mouth grim and cold. Blue eyes filled with disgust swept from Van to Leigh.

Leigh caught her breath—there was no mistaking the well-known face of Matt Hunter.

This was her boss.

2
____

Oh, no, Leigh thought aghast.

What must he think of her? She should have been getting a good night's sleep before starting a strange job early the following morning, but it would look to him as if she was about to do the very opposite. What a way to meet her boss for the first time!

Inwardly, she groaned.

Van cleared his throat. 'I can explain everything, Matt,' he said, and he took a step towards him.

But Matt Hunter was not looking at his PA—he was looking at Leigh, contempt on his face.

'I apologise for being out here so late,' Van began again. 'We—'

The actor gestured for him to stop.

'You'd no right to bring a woman out here in my absence, and certainly not at this time of night. And not for what you were obviously planning to do,' he said icily.

Van flushed. 'It's not—' he began.

'Save it for the morning, Van,' Matt Hunter cut in. 'I want

the woman off the premises at once. We'll talk about this tomorrow.'

He turned and walked out, leaving the door wide open.

Leigh glanced nervously at Van. His face was ashen. For a second, she thought she saw white fury spark in his eyes. But if she had, it was instantly gone.

'I must apologise to you, Leigh,' he said stiffly, moving to the doorway, and indicating that she should go through it.

'First for bringing you out here so late, and then for Matt's rudeness. If he'd thought at all, he'd have realised that you were the new secretary. You had a great deal to learn in a short amount of time so it's not that surprising we were working late. But he's a lot on his mind, and he just didn't think.'

'That's understandable,' she said. She paused while Van locked the cabana door behind them, and then they started walking in silence towards the house.

Anxiety churned in her stomach.

Van had seemed distinctly put out in the face of his boss's rudeness, and at the conclusion Matt Hunter had jumped to, and she hated to think that relations between her and Van might have been soured because of that.

Apart from the fact that she was bound to need his help when Tom left, it would be so much more pleasant if all those living in the house got on well with each other.

When they reached the house, Van slid open the glass doors and gestured for her to go inside.

'I imagine you're not too sure of the way,' he said. 'It's all still very new to you, and there are several corridors. I'll point you towards your room, and then say goodnight.' And then, as if reading her mind, he added with a reassuring smile, 'You've no need to look so worried, Leigh. Things will be all right tomorrow. You'll see.'

He took her to the end of the corridor, indicated her bedroom and left her.

She went into her room, closed the door and leaned back against it, listening to the sound of Van's footsteps as they died away in the distance.

For some unaccountable reason, she shivered with apprehension.

3

———

The alarm was shrill in the silence of the room.

Leigh woke with a jolt. She stretched out her arm, switched off the alarm, sat up in bed and glanced at her bedside clock—seven o'clock.

She'd an hour before she started work. She'd forgotten to find out when she should go for her breakfast and where, but she wouldn't have been able to eat a thing anyway, so she'd go straight to Matt Hunter's study when she was ready.

The most important thing now was to be sure of making the right impression, and that began with not being late.

She flung back the sheet, jumped out of bed and went quickly into the shower room. Too nervous to revel in the sense of the luxury of the room with its sweep of white tiles and glass, she threw off her baggy T-shirt, stepped into the shower and under the powerful flow of water, stood for a few minutes letting the water course through her hair and down her body. Then she soaped herself and shampooed her hair.

Minutes later, she stepped from the shower, tingling all over.

Grabbing a soft white bath sheet from the pile of towels on one of the glass shelves, she dried herself. Then she took another towel from the pile, towel-dried the worst of the damp from her hair and reached for her brush and hairdryer.

Her hair, when left to dry on its own, soon became a tangle of unruly auburn curls. But that wasn't the look she was aiming for that morning, so she'd made sure that she'd have sufficient time to dry her hair properly before she faced her new employer.

As she replaced the hairdryer, she glanced at her reflection in the mirror.

The face that stared back at her was pale beneath its light golden tan, and the large hazel eyes lacked their customary sparkle. Hardly surprising, she thought, since all she could feel was dread at the thought of meeting someone who, only hours before, had assumed that she was about to sleep with one of his other employees, a man she'd only just met.

Her clothes that morning had to spell out efficiency and commitment, and undo the negative impression she'd given the night before, she decided firmly as she returned to the bedroom and went into her walk-in closet. Sombre and severe were going to be her watchwords.

That ruled out all her minis for a start!

Her gaze ran along the rails, and stopped at her beige linen dress. She pulled it from the rail and held it up. Cap sleeves and a high neck. Unrelieved beige from the neckline to the hem, which came just above her knees.

Bingo!

The dress screamed efficiency, and with its chin-hugging neckline, was so far from sexy that it would spell out loud and clear to her boss that she had no designs on anyone in the house.

How lucky that on more than one occasion she'd resisted the urge to bin that boring dress, she thought as she wriggled into it, and also that she'd included it among the few things she'd packed when she'd briefly returned to her apartment the day before.

She zipped up the back, checked her appearance in the full-length mirror, confirmed that it was dullness itself, and returned to the bedroom.

Picking up her bag and notebook, she went across to the door. Taking a deep breath to steady her nerves, she opened the door, walked out of the room and went along the corridor towards the part of the house where, if she remembered correctly, she'd find Matt Hunter's study.

'Why the hell are you still here?' Matt Hunter's fist pounded hard on his large mahogany desk, and he rose to his feet. 'I thought I told you last night to get out,' he thundered at her as she hovered in the doorway.

'You misunderstood the situation last night, Mr Hunter,' she began. She heard the tremor in her voice, and cleared her throat. 'Van was showing me around. He'd just finished and we were about to go back to the house.'

'Of course.' His voice dripped with sarcasm. 'That's why there were two full glasses of wine on the table.'

She swallowed anxiously. 'I can explain what happened.' She inched further into the room.

'And so can I!' he snapped, sitting down. 'But I don't need to. The scene rather spoke for itself, wouldn't you say? It was gone midnight and it was dark. You were alone with Van, and you were drinking.'

She took a step forward.

'And as I assume that Van didn't carry you screaming through the gardens while the rest of my staff were afflicted by a sudden deafness,' he went on, 'your presence there must have been out of choice.'

'You've got it all wrong,' she said, exasperation building up. 'I wasn't with Van in the way you mean. And nor was it actually that dark, if you think about it. There was a moon up there and a sky full of stars. Not to mention spotlights in the garden. I went out there with Van because—'

'Because you thought that if you did, he'd get you into the movies,' he cut in wearily. 'Girls like you are a dime a dozen. They go after me, after Van, after everyone close to me. But you won't get anything that way. Van shouldn't have brought you here—and I'll deal with that—but now...' He paused, and straightened up. 'Hey! Where did you sleep last night?'

His face filled with sudden rage.

She stamped her foot, and glared at him. 'For heavens' sake, will you let me speak! If you'd be kind enough to do so, I could tell you. I slept in what'll be my room for as long as I'm here. I'm working for you. I'm Leigh Carter, your temporary secretary.'

He gave a start of surprise.

'No, you're not! Tom hired a man.'

'No, he didn't—he hired *me*. Or rather he and Van did. Van spent most of yesterday, including the evening, showing me around and telling me what I needed to know.'

'Leigh's a man's name.'

'Not exclusively, it isn't. If you give me a minute, I'm sure I can come up with some well-known Leighs who're women.' She paused. 'And anyway, does it matter that I'm a female?'

'I prefer to have a male secretary. I'm working on a complex deal at the moment, and that's not the sort of work for a woman. I'm sure there're many excellent female secretaries around, but they're not for me. I'm used to working with a man, and that's the way I want it to stay.'

'That sounds very sexist!'

'Well, it's not—it's just being practical. I'm wary of working with women outside of the movies. It's because of how they can behave towards me.' A defensive look spread over his face. 'I'm sorry about the way that makes me sound, but it's the truth.'

'I suppose I can understand that,' she said grudgingly.

And she could. The light that fell through the glass doors into the study was highlighting the planes of the face in front of her. Even scowling, he was quite the most attractive man she'd ever seen.

Then a sudden thought struck her, and her brow creased in bewilderment.

'Wait a minute, though!' She went further into the room. 'The agency sent you my photo as well as my details. It was probably a bit grainy, but you'd still have been able to see me. How many men have shoulder length auburn curls and wear lipstick?'

'You'd be surprised how many,' he said tetchily. 'This is Hollywood, after all. But I take your point.' He shifted in his chair. 'To be honest, I didn't look at the stuff the agency sent. I hadn't time—I had to go out. We needed someone who could start at once, and the agency gave us one name only— yours. I told Tom and Van to interview you and decide, but said that if you weren't right, they weren't to take you. We'd have gone back to the agency rather than that. Tom didn't tell me you were a woman.'

His tone accused her.

'I think you'll find that although I'm female, I've got the right qualifications and have superior skills. I've worked for a film production company in the past, so I'm used to the speed and jargon of the media, and, amazingly, I'm used to complex deals, too. The fact that I've worked non-stop in LA since the day I put my name on the agency books speaks for itself, if I may use your words.'

He glared at her.

'I'm well up to the job, which is what matters after all, and I'm here now,' she went on quickly, trying to sound more confident than she felt as she stood in the chill that emanated from her boss's clear blue eyes. 'I'll get my CV for you if you'd like,' she added, and she attempted a smile.

He shook his head. 'That won't be necessary. As you say, you're here now, and Tom's gotta get off this morning. I'm gonna have to give you a try.' He hesitated. 'I guess I got one or two things wrong, Miss Carter, and I might've spoken out of line. Since it seems we're gonna be working together, it might be an idea to start with a clean sheet.'

'It's kind of you to apologise,' she said in surprise. 'And I'm sorry if I was rude to you just now. I might have been a bit snappy. And I'm sorry I stamped my foot. I don't usually do things like that.'

'Apology accepted.' He gestured to her to go to the chair. 'You *can* sit down, you know. The chair on the other side of my desk is a clue that there's no need to stay standing.'

'Thank you,' she said, swallowing a sharp retort as she walked across the polished wooden floor, which was strewn with dramatically patterned rugs, and sat down on the chair.

She looked quickly around the room, and then back at Matt Hunter, who'd started separating the papers on his desk into piles. From the small amount of time she'd spent with him, she knew that she was going to need every ounce of her self-control if she was to keep her job.

No matter how rude he was, and she was sure that no matter what he'd just said, he would be rude to her again, she absolutely mustn't answer him back.

'I'll be going out soon,' he told her, glancing up. 'Tom doesn't leave till midday. He'll be here soon and he'll take you into his office and fill you in on anything Van might have missed. Van will have told you the basics, but Tom needs to show you his way of doing things.'

'Of course.'

He picked up a black leather bag and put some of the papers into it.

He seemed cool and very much in control, she thought enviously, in lightweight stone-coloured chinos and an open-necked shirt in a deep cornflower blue. He'd rolled his sleeves back to the elbows, revealing strong tanned forearms.

Sadly, she must look the opposite, she realised. Despite her efforts with a hairdryer, her hair was bound to be curling all over the place by now, and her pure linen dress was already more wrinkled than the hide of an ancient rhinoceros.

Too late she remembered why she'd intended to bin it. The last of the confidence her dress had given her was fast evaporating.

He looked up from his desk. The blue of his shirt rivalled the deep blue of his eyes, she couldn't help noticing.

'While you're waiting for Tom, and only if it's not too exhausting, given you can't have had much sleep last night,' he said with an obviously feigned concern, 'I could use a coffee.' He waved his arm in the direction of wooden doors at the back of the room. 'There's a bar behind the doors. I take it black. I assume that's within your range of superior skills.'

Enough was enough!

'Clean sheet, you said!' she exploded. 'Well, you seem to have torn it up pretty fast! It's well within my range, Mr Hunter. But what about your range of skills, if I may ask? Do they include the ability to be polite to people? I'm asking because you seem to be so used to considering only yourself that you don't feel any need to consider others.'

He gave a sharp exclamation.

'But actually, you do,' she continued, undaunted. 'It's not that difficult to be pleasant, you know—you really should try it some time. If it helps, you could pretend you're rehearsing for a role in a film—that of being mister nice guy.'

'What!' He sat bolt upright, his eyes glinting ominously.

'Oh, I see! You're asking me what you should say in order to come across as pleasant. Well, for example, you could ask if I have everything I need...'

He rose from his chair and leaned forward, his fists on his desk, his knuckles white. She went on relentlessly.

'And now that we've established why I'm here, you could ask if my room was comfortable, my breakfast okay—if I've had any breakfast, for that matter, or any coffee. Anything that shows a concern for the well being of your staff is called consideration. If you tried it, you might even get to like the way it made you feel.'

'Have you quite finished, Miss Carter?' he said, his tone steely. He sat back down, scowling.

'No, actually, I haven't. I know there was a misunderstanding about what I was doing here. I thought we'd got over that, though, but I was obviously wrong. It might be that you're still angry that I'm a woman,' she continued. 'Can't help you with that, I'm afraid.'

'If I might speak,' he said, slowly and deliberately.

'I've not quite finished. Living in someone else's house isn't easy and you should be going out of your way to make me feel comfortable. Instead, you're doing the opposite.' She sat back in her chair and stared defiantly across the desk. 'Now I've finished.'

'Then it's my turn.' He frowned at her. 'This may be a novel idea for you, Miss Carter, being from li'l old England and all that, but here in the States, what the boss says goes. And I'm the boss.'

'Being the boss doesn't give you the right to be rude,' she retorted.

'Hey, it's my turn now—you've had your say! As I was saying when you so *rudely* interrupted me—as I'm the boss, and you're the employee, you're here to take care of me, to worry about what *I* need. Not the other way round. Now if you don't like that, I can go back to the agency, and so can you.'

Alarm shot through Leigh. Go back to the agency? Not a chance! That was not going to happen!

Although she felt that she had the upper hand, she didn't dare to call what could be a bluff, just in case he was serious. She was desperate to keep the job, no matter how unpleasant her employer.

She swallowed hard.

'I'm sorry, Mr Hunter,' she said, hanging her head and assuming a tone of great remorse. 'I do apologise for what I just said—it was unforgivable of me.'

He gave a short grunt. 'Well, maybe I was also a bit rude,' he muttered.

She opened her mouth.

'Okay, very rude,' he said with a hint of a smile. 'I'm sorry about that. But in my defence, this is a real stressful time. Tom having to leave so suddenly has thrown me.'

'Of course,' she murmured.

'I'm about to take over a small film company and Tom has been involved from the start. The next few weeks would have been difficult whether or not he was here, and they're going to be even harder now. But I'm sure you'll cope,' he added quickly.

He leaned back stared at Leigh.

There was a definite hint of amusement in his eyes, she saw, and she felt a degree of relief. It seemed as if any immediate threat to her job had passed.

'Tell me, are you typical of all the gals who come from London, England, or did I just luck out?'

'I think you'll have to blame my red hair, not where I was born,' she said lightly.

He gave her a smile, and then he leaned forward to speak into the intercom. Her pulse quickened. He should smile more often.

'Tom, could you come along now? And when you've run through the last of the things Miss Carter needs to know before you leave, you must get off.'

Matt released the button on the intercom and relaxed.

There was a sound at the side of the room. Turning her head, she saw that Tom Grover had come through a door at the window end of the room. He looked tired and drawn, and as if he could use a cup of coffee, she thought as he came towards her. And he wasn't the only one.

She was suddenly aware that she hadn't yet had her morning caffeine fix. She tried to remember when she'd last had a coffee. It must've been early evening the day before.

No wonder she wasn't yet on top of things, and had let her tongue run away with her.

Tom glanced at the desk. 'I'll get you a coffee, Matt, before I take Leigh off with me,' he said, and he went across to the wooden doors at the back of the room. Moments later, the tempting aroma of coffee reached her. Perhaps they'd all have a cup, she thought, and her spirits rose.

But when Tom emerged from the concealed bar, he was carrying one cup only, which he put down in front of Matt Hunter, before going to sit at the side of the desk.

She couldn't stop herself from giving a small gasp of disappointment.

Matt Hunter looked up sharply.

With difficulty, she tore her eyes from his cup of steaming black coffee, and fixed them on the patterned rug that hung on the wall behind him.

He followed her gaze. 'It's a ceremonial rug,' he told her, picking up his cup. 'It was made by Navajo women. If you hold it up to the light, you can see little holes where the women occasionally dropped a stitch. They weren't perfect either.'

To which of them was he referring, she wondered, but she decided not to ask.

He took a second sip. His eyes on Leigh's face, he gave an exaggerated sigh of pleasure. She pressed her lips together to keep herself from physically drooling.

He finished his coffee, pushed the cup away, picked up his leather bag and stood up. The shadow of a smile played across his lips as he glanced down at Leigh.

'Put her out of her misery, Tom. Get her a coffee and have one yourself. And call Conchita. Ask her to bring some pastries along. I suspect Miss Carter hasn't had any breakfast yet.'

'Thank you, Mr Hunter,' she said with a grateful smile.

'You're welcome.' He moved round to the front of his desk. 'I must go now—I've an appointment at the studio. You'll find it in the diary. Tom will show you where he keeps the diary. Any problems after Tom's gone, see Van.'

Her heart sank at the mention of Van. She was in no hurry to see him again.

She wouldn't easily forget the humiliation on Van's face when Matt had ordered him to see her off the premises, and had then turned his back on Van, and walked out.

Van could quite easily resent her as a result, and if he did, he might decide not to help her any more than he had to.

'Touch base regularly, Tom, and let us know how things are going at home.' Matt's words cut into her thoughts. 'And show Leigh where she'll have lunch. If you see a young girl around, Leigh, it'll be Conchita's daughter, Maria,' he added. 'She's a cute kid.'

Two cups of coffee and two Danish pastries later, Tom had outlined Leigh's duties to her and shown her where everything was, and they were relaxing in the last few minutes before he had to leave for the airport.

'You'll be first class,' he told her. 'Now, is there anything else you want to know?'

'Mr Hunter said something—'

Tom stopped her. 'I should've told you before—it's Matt, not Mr Hunter. We're informal here. He's been calling you Miss Carter because you've only just arrived.'

'Mr ... Matt mentioned a business deal.'

'That's right. He's buying a small movie company called Heartlands. You'll have some documents to type, but Van will do anything heavier than that—he's now up to speed with all the details. And I might even be back before matters come to a head.'

'Isn't it unusual for an actor to be buying companies, even if they're to do with films?'

'It's not as unusual as it used to be. And Matt's ambitious. A while back, he lost a lot of money in a scandal involving his manager and accountants. Since then, he's supervised all his investments and he's found it real interesting. This is his first attempt at buying a production company, though, so it's particularly important for him.'

'Why does he want the company?'

'To have a greater say over the films he makes, and over the films that get made. I'm sure he'll also be looking at buying books that could be made into films.'

'I see.'

'But as far as you're concerned, apart from tabulating the market's closing figures in certain areas of investment, and making notes during any meetings he has, you're unlikely to be involved with the business side of things. That's Van's province.'

'Will I be house based?'

'For most of the time, yes. But occasionally you'll ago with Matt to the studio or a business meeting.' He paused, and looked around. 'Now, can you think of anything I might have missed?'

'Not a thing. You've been really thorough. I'm very grateful to you.'

'If anything awkward crops up, ask Van. And Matt will always help, but he's often out.'

'Is he making a film at the moment?'

'He finished one not so long ago. He's re-shooting some

scenes for it now. And he's doing some pre-production work for the next film.'

'Do you mind me asking if there's a woman in his life?'

'I can't say for certain as he's a very private man, but I'm pretty sure there isn't.'

'That's surprising, isn't it?'

'Not really. I imagine he's nervous about getting involved with anyone. He went through a difficult divorce some years ago, and as a result, he hardly sees his daughter. That hurts real bad as he's very fond of Carey.'

'That must be awful.'

Tom nodded. 'It is. What makes it harder for someone like Matt is that it's difficult for him to be able to share his feelings. He never knows if it's his success that's drawn the woman, or if she genuinely likes him as a person. There are so many women in Hollywood just out to meet someone with money, or someone who can get them on to the screen.'

'His ex wife was an actress, wasn't she?'

'That's right. Cybill Harding. Not the easiest of women. She was bigger than he was when they met, but not any longer. I believe she's still quite popular in Italy, but her career in the States is virtually over.'

'What about Van? How long has he worked for Matt?'

'For years. They majored in drama at UCLA at the same time and became great friends. Matt hasn't any close family left, and in vacations he and Van would go off to Mexico and stay with some of Van's distant relatives who live there. They both got parts in films after drama school, and apparently Van, too, was a good actor. He got several small parts in B-movies, but it was Matt who got the big break. He starred in a low budget movie called *Love Be Good*, and to everyone's amazement, it became a huge success. The rest is history.'

'What about Van?'

Tom shrugged. 'He never got the break he needed. Matt managed to get him a part in a couple of films, but Van's career just didn't take off.'

So Matt Hunter wasn't too big to help out an old friend.

Her new boss was a strange mixture.

He'd been rude to her, yes. But she'd been rude to him back, and he hadn't sacked her. He'd been annoyed with her, it was true—but he *was* the boss, so he actually had a right to be annoyed at the manner in which she'd spoken to him.

And it had been kind of amusing, the way he'd drunk his coffee, sort of teasing her as he did so, and had then made sure that she had something to eat and drink before he left. And she didn't really think it was just because she'd lectured him on how to behave.

No, she couldn't make up her mind what she thought about him. Fortunately, though, she didn't have to come to decision—she just had to get on with him in a working relationship for the short amount of time that she'd be helping him out.

'Is there a problem, Leigh?' Tom asked. 'You're frowning.'

'Was I? I didn't realise. I was just thinking about what you were saying about Van's lack of success.'

'You see it all the time, good actors who don't get anywhere. There are so many talented actors in Hollywood that you need luck as well as talent. Van didn't have Matt's luck, and when he hit the bottom of the barrel, Matt gave him a home and a job here, and his own office. The job was somewhat manufactured for Van, to be honest, but it's worked well, and it means the secretary isn't overloaded. So Van's both an employee and a close friend. Matt's one of the good guys, Leigh, as you'll find out for yourself.'

.   .   .

AFTER LEIGH HAD SEEN Tom off to the airport, she returned to her office and sat down behind her desk.

She looked around the pleasant, airy room, and ran her hand along the top of her desk, which was a smaller version of her boss's mahogany desk. Then she leaned back and gazed at the view through the large glass doors, which she faced.

It was going to be very easy to work in such a place, she thought, even though her office was slightly closer to Matt Hunter's study than she'd have liked.

Impulsively, she got up, went across to the glass doors and pulled them apart. Letting them slide into the wall on either side, she stepped out into the midday sun. As she did so, a sudden movement caught her eye, and she turned in time to see a tiny green lizard dart up the outside wall.

Mesmerised by its grace, she stood very still and watched it. Halfway up the wall, it paused, turned its unblinking gaze towards her, and then ran back down the wall at speed, and disappeared into a crack.

Smiling to herself, she strolled to the edge of the terrace and stared out at the garden.

Even though her boss might turn out to be quite difficult to work for, it sounded as if the job was always going to be interesting, and that there'd be a degree of variety in what she did. And that was a huge plus point.

Fran would be dead envious when she told her about it, which she would have to do before too long or she'd find herself having to look for a new best friend!

Once she was familiar with the routine of her week, and knew when she'd be free, she'd give Fran a call and arrange to meet her for a good catch-up over lunch.

The downside of living-in was going to be that she wouldn't be able to do what she did with the agency—book the occasional few hours off so that she and Fran could trawl through the shops together, or meet somewhere for an extended lunch. She'd miss that freedom. But it was going to be worth it, both for the interesting variety the job was going to offer, and for the financial rewards.

'How are you settling in, Leigh?'

She gave a start of surprise and spun round. Van was standing on the terrace behind her.

'Gosh, you made me jump, Van,' she said, and she laughed with embarrassment.

'I hope you found everything you needed.'

'I did. Between you and Tom, it would've been impossible not to have done so. I'm very grateful for all your help yesterday.'

'You're welcome. It was a pleasure.'

She felt herself colour slightly. 'I do feel uncomfortable about Mr Hunter getting the wrong idea last night, though, and I'd like to apologise for my part in it.'

He lifted a slender finger to silence her.

'You've nothing to apologise for. If anything, *I* should be apologising to *you*. I was so anxious to tell you everything I could about the job that I didn't appreciate how tired you must be, nor how inappropriate it was for us to be out there by ourselves at that time of night. I'm not surprised that Matt jumped to the wrong conclusion. But *I* was at fault, not you.'

'It's very kind of you to say so, but I still feel guilty.'

'It's in the past and forgotten. Are we agreed?' He raised an eyebrow.

'If you're sure?'

'I am. We'll shake on it.' He held out his hand and she

took it with a smile. 'Now I suggest we ring Conchita and ask her to bring your lunch out here. After lunch, you can spend the rest of the afternoon getting to know your office. I've got to go downtown now, but I'll be back before you need to tabulate the stock market figures, and I'll go through that with you.'

'That would be terrific; thank you.'

'Tom and I usually eat with Matt in the evenings if he's at home. Unless he has guests, of course. When I don't have dinner with Matt, I prefer to eat on my own. I always have work to catch up with, and I tend to read while I eat.'

'Of course.'

'Since Matt will be out this evening, we could ask Conchita to serve you an early meal. Then you can have a good night's sleep.'

'Thank you, Van. That's really considerate of you.'

Relief flooded through her. Everything was going to be fine after all.

4

———

Van Attwood walked steadily across the wide drive to the garage block.

So Miss Leigh Carter really thought he was being considerate, did she? And she truly believed that he'd completely put behind him the humiliation he'd suffered the night before. A humiliation she'd brought about. How naïve! It was going to take something far stronger than a mere apology to erase the anger he felt towards her.

Justifiable anger.

That uptight teasing bitch.

What had she expected him to think the night before, the way she'd been behaving towards him throughout the day?

She'd been all over him, and in the evening, too, in a way that was far more friendly than you'd expect of any job applicant.

He'd never have suggested going to the cabana at that time of night if he hadn't been certain, as a result of the exceptional warmth she'd shown him, that she was up for some action.

The cabana had seemed the best destination for what he'd had in mind. Any activity in her bedroom or his would have felt too close to Matt Hunter for comfort. But the cabana, being away from the house, would allow them to escape the stifling sense of his overarching presence.

And she'd gone readily enough into the garden with him after dark, hadn't she?

He hadn't had to force her.

There'd been nothing to tell him that he'd misread the situation. Or at least, not until they'd almost reached the cabana, and then it hadn't been much of a protest—it had seemed more of a way of trying to avoid looking too willing rather than anything else.

To then go and make it clear, after he was fully aroused, that the word goodnight was all he was going to get!

The unbelievable nerve!

He deserved better than that.

He'd actually let himself believe that she was interested in him as a person, and that she wasn't like every other woman he seemed to meet—playing up to him, pretending to like him, but before long letting it slip that she saw him only as a means of getting to the glittering prize.

Since she was going to work for the glittering prize, anyway, she'd had no reason to play up to him in order to achieve that goal. But play up she had, and that had raised his hopes that in the short amount of time they'd known each other, she'd come to feel something for him.

But he'd been so very wrong.

It was now obvious that as soon as she'd felt secure about having the job, he'd served his purpose.

She was clearly just another woman who'd set her sights on the actor. When the time came that she was alone with Matt Hunter, she'd no doubt play up to him, too. But she wouldn't be calling a halt before he'd even reached first base. No way!

Of course, as it turned out, it was just as well that he hadn't gone as far with her as he'd intended, given that Matt had returned much sooner than expected.

It was a matter of great luck that he'd heard the sound of someone outside the cabana, and had swiftly reined himself in and redeemed the situation as best he could before the door opened.

Bile had risen in his throat as he'd had to deliver an abject apology to a tease who should've been apologising to him for the way she'd led him on.

He'd been humiliated in front of Matt, thanks to her. And he wasn't going to forget that in a hurry.

In all fairness to Matt, it wasn't exactly surprising, given the location and the time of day, that Matt had jumped to the conclusion he had. But it *was* surprising that he'd felt the need to be as rude as he'd been.

He had been unnecessarily rude. Unforgivably so.

The cheek of it! And in front of a mere temp. He'd never before been so embarrassed.

Even if Matt had been right in what he'd assumed, he shouldn't have spoken to an old friend in such a contemptuous way. Success had clearly gone to Matt Hunter's head and made him forget that he, too, was a man with human failings.

He'd been thinking for a while that his boss needed to be taken down a peg or two, and last night had confirmed it.

He was going to pay for his arrogance.

And Leigh Carter was going to pay, too.

She must pay for the position she'd got him into the night before, and for falsely getting his hopes up in the way she had.

Both of them would answer for the humiliation he'd suffered at their hands. That was a promise.

Just how he'd make them pay, he didn't yet know. But Tom would be gone for at least a couple of weeks, possibly even longer, so he'd got time to give this some thought.

Ideally, the perfect opportunity would present itself, and if it did so, he'd be ready.

But if it didn't, he was sure that he'd be able to find a way of giving a helping hand to any situation with potential.

Whatever he hit them with, he'd see that it hurt.

5

———

Leigh stared mesmerised through the tinted windows of the car as Conchita's husband, Armando, drove her and Matt Hunter through the palm tree lined streets of Los Angeles.

Seen at speed, LA was a city of identical girls: all gleaming gold, size zero, long blonde hair and slim legs. It was a city without cellulite. She gave an involuntary tug on her skirt.

Her choice of clothes for that day had once again been a mistake.

When she'd got up, she'd had no idea that on her second day only in the job she'd be going out with her boss.

To look the epitome of competence, not comfort, had been her aim when she'd gazed along the limited choice on her clothes rail that morning, and she'd selected a short straight grey cotton skirt and a white blouse, rather than a dress or slacks.

Feeling that a touch of make-up would enhance the look of seriousness engendered by her clothes, she'd run an eye pencil along her eyelids just above her eyelashes, and had given herself a touch of lipstick for colour.

She'd had breakfast at seven, gone into the study at eight on the dot, and had found Matt, leather case in hand, looking as if he was about to go out.

'I'd like you to come to the studio with me,' he'd said, and she'd had time only to grab a notebook and throw a few things in her bag before they left.

As the car had driven off, she'd glanced down at her lap. Her skirt had slid upwards, and an expanse of thigh was on view.

She glanced anxiously at Matt, but fortunately he was too engrossed in the *Wall Street Journal* to have noticed.

She pulled at the skirt and put her notebook squarely on her lap. Fervently wishing she'd brought a larger notebook, she wriggled in her seat, trying to get into a better position, and tugged again at her skirt.

Matt folded his newspaper with an exasperated sigh. 'Is this dance routine something I'm going to have to get used to if I want to do any work on a journey?' he asked, his voice heavy with weariness. 'I thought I'd dictate a few notes. But only if you're sitting comfortably.'

Not that engrossed, then.

'I'm sorry for disturbing you. And I'm comfortable now, thank you, Mr Hunter,' she replied quickly, and she dug in her bag for a pencil. 'Ready when you are.'

Positioning herself, her pencil poised, she waited for him to begin.

Silence.

Why didn't he start, she wondered, squashing the urge to pull at her skirt again. She glanced at him and saw that he was staring at her hand.

'Do you normally take notes with an eyebrow pencil,

Miss Carter, or at least that's what I think that instrument is? If so, it must be another quaint British custom with which I've so far not been familiar.'

'I'm so sorry,' she said. To her horror, she felt herself going scarlet as she thrust the pencil hastily back into her bag. 'I do apologise.'

'I'd rather not hear the word "sorry" again. That goes for today, tomorrow and for the rest of your stay. I think we'll take it as read that you've now apologised not only for past and present mistakes, but also for all the mistakes I suspect you're going to make in the future.'

She smiled in apology. 'I'm afraid I seem to be jinxed at the moment.'

'I can't disagree with that.'

'But that's the last of it, I assure you,' she said brightly, swapping her pen for her eyebrow pencil. 'I'm ready now, so fire away.'

She gave a surreptitious tug on her skirt.

'Perhaps fire is not the best choice of verb in the circumstances,' he murmured. 'There's a rug behind you. It might serve your purpose. And then maybe we can begin.'

Sarcastic beast, she thought, reaching for the rug and spreading it over her knees.

Checking that her pen was facing the right direction—she wasn't going to be wrong-footed a second time!—she nodded her readiness for him to start, and he did.

WITH DOWNTOWN LOS ANGELES far behind them, the studio came into sight. When they reached the iron gates at the entrance, Armando slowed the limousine sufficiently for the uniformed guard to recognise Matt, and then he drove through the gates into the huge complex. A few minutes later, he brought the car to a halt in front of a block of single storey offices.

Matt and Leigh got out, and Leigh followed Matt to one of the low white buildings.

'This is where my meeting is,' Matt said, stopping in front of the entrance. 'There's no need for you to come in with me. In fact, I'd rather you went to the Publicity Department. It's only over there.' He pointed to a building two blocks away. 'It'd be a sight more helpful if you sorted out a few stills that could be sent to folk who write in for a signed photo.'

She stared at him in amazement. 'Don't you want to choose your own photos, decide what makes you look best and so on?'

'Not really. Most of the fans who write in are women, and since I'm now stuck with a female secretary, I might as well make the most of it. You're a woman so you'll know what appeals to women. If you see such a photo, choose it.'

'That's a tall order. I might have to come away empty-handed.' Her hand flew to her mouth. 'Ouch! I shouldn't have said that—actors thrive on flattery!' She put her hand to her head. 'Oh, God, I shouldn't have said that, either.'

Matt Hunter raised his eyebrows slightly.

For a moment, Leigh wondered if she'd seen a glint of amusement flicker in his eyes, but the blue gaze that enveloped her was one of steely control.

'When you're in a hole, Miss Carter,' he said evenly, 'it's advisable to stop digging.'

'Believe me, the spade's now locked in the gardening shed,' she said fervently.

'And when you've selected some photos,' he continued, 'always assuming the task doesn't prove impossible, you can take a look round the studio if you like.'

'Oh, I'd really like that!'

'Don't get too excited! There are few full-length films shot here these days, I'm afraid. Studios are in desperate need of dollars so now they rent out the lots for commercials and TV series. And there's a great deal of admin done here. But there's quite a bit of this studio that's been left as it was in its heyday, and you might find that interesting. I'll send someone to show you around.'

'I'd love that! Thank you so much,' she said in excitement, and she turned slightly to look at the large grey hangar-like buildings flanking the wide road that led further into the studio complex.

Feeling his eyes on the side of her face, she looked back at him and smiled happily.

'On second thoughts,' he said, a trace of awkwardness in his voice, 'I don't think I'm needed for anything after the meeting, and if I'm not, I'll show you around myself. I'll come across to Publicity when I'm done. If I find that I'll be tied up after all, I'll send someone else in my place.'

He nodded to her, went into the building and closed the door behind him.

THE MORNING PASSED SWIFTLY.

It hadn't been hard to find suitable photos—the camera loved him. The difficulty had been in sticking to the small number of different shots required. But she finally made her choice, gave her selection to the people in Publicity, and as they were packing everything away, a phone call to Publicity told her that Matt was on his way.

Perfect timing, she thought as she stepped outside and saw him walking towards her.

How did he do it, she wondered in envy.

It was a hot day, and now that she was away from the air-conditioning, she felt herself rapidly wilting. But despite her boss being in a pale grey suit—albeit a lightweight one, and with a white shirt that was open at the neck—he was managing to look very cool.

And very attractive.

In fact, if he hadn't been her boss, and prone to an irritability he kept hidden from his fans, she could almost have fancied him herself.

'Did you get them sorted, Miss Carter?' he asked when he reached her.

'I did. I hope you approve the ones I picked.'

'I'm sure I will. Right then; let's take a look at the studio, shall we? Where would you like to start?'

'With food. I'm starving.'

He grinned at her. 'Those are words that aren't often heard inside a studio. I'm kinda hungry, too, so the canteen it is, then.'

After a short wait in the canteen queue, they reached the front of the line. Matt got them each a pastrami on rye sandwich and a coffee, and led the way to a table next to the window.

Almost as soon as they'd sat down, he excused himself, and went across to a nearby table and spoke to a young man with a deep tan and a shock of sun-bleached hair that fell across his forehead.

She looked curiously around the canteen.

It wasn't at all what she'd expected by way of appearance, with its very ordinary Formica topped tables and plastic seated chairs. But the people eating at the tables looked far from ordinary.

There was every shape and size, some in nightclothes,

some in daywear and some in formal evening dress. And many wore extravagant colourful costumes.

Two women at a table across the room particularly caught her eye, and she watched, feeling as nervous on their behalf as they must feel for themselves, as each of them struggled to stand up while keeping a huge feathered head-dress balanced upright on her head.

She heard Matt sit down, turned her attention back to the table, picked up her sandwich again and bit into it.

'I'm sorry about that,' he said. 'I was talking to Chuck Bourassa. He's the one who would've shown you around if I hadn't been able to. I've asked him to leave one of the studio Jeeps outside, and we'll take that—it's too hot to attempt to see everything on foot. You'd be amazed at the size of the lots.'

'Is Chuck an actor, too?'

'Yes, but he's resting, as they say. There are weekday tours of the studio, and he's been driving the tour bus while he waits for a break. He also works as a waiter on La Cienega. He's a nice kid. I hope he gets something before too long.'

She went to take another bite of her sandwich, but stopped, feeling the strange sensation of being watched.

Glancing quickly around, she saw that their table was, indeed, the object of attention, but it was Matt they were looking at, not her, although she was at the receiving end of one or two curious glances.

Matt seemed to be a magnet for the eyes of every woman nearby, yet he appeared to be completely unaware of the effect he was having, and was focused solely on what he was eating.

For a moment or two, she stared at the top of the head

that was looking down at his food. Yes, magnetism was the right word, she thought, and she returned to her meal.

'Is the sandwich okay?' he asked a few moments later.

'It's more than okay, thank you. And I love the gherkins.'

'You don't know what a change it is to eat with a woman who does more than nibble a lettuce leaf. I've even known women to eat one prawn and say they're full. One prawn, I ask you! It's no fun having a meal with someone like that.'

'Then prepare yourself for an excess of fun—I don't intend to waste a single crumb.'

Matt smiled at her, and continued eating.

When they'd finished their sandwiches and coffee, he glanced at his watch. 'If you're ready, we'll get going. There's a lot to see.'

She clapped her hands. 'Top marks for your play on the word lot.'

He looked at her questioningly, and then his brow cleared and he smiled.

'It was deliberate, of course,' he said, grinning.

They both laughed.

Blinking furiously as they went out into the bright sun, Leigh followed Matt across the dusty road to a small open Jeep. He got in behind the wheel.

'Jump in,' he told her.

She climbed in beside him, and he started to drive along a road that had enormous grey warehouse-type structures on either side. Suddenly, he swung the Jeep to the right and stopped sharply.

'Take a look at that,' he said.

'Why, it's Main Street!' she exclaimed in delight. 'It's where all the gunfights in cowboy films take place.'

'It sure is.' He started the Jeep again, and drove slowly

between worn facades of wooden houses, shops, banks and swinging-door saloons.

'Why's everything so much smaller than normal?'

'To make the actors look taller. Some of them were quite a bit shorter than you would've thought.'

THE AFTERNOON PASSED AS SWIFTLY AS HAD the morning, and the sun's rays were beginning to lengthen as Matt pulled up in front of a wooden bridge spanning a man-made lake. He climbed out and told Leigh to get down, too.

'We're leaving the Jeep here, and walking the rest of the way—some places are better approached on foot. Chuck knows where he'll find the buggy. When we get over the bridge, we're gonna turn into a street that you can't see from here.'

'Hm. That sounds intriguing.'

He glanced enigmatically at her, but didn't say a word, and together they strolled over the bridge, and then turned right.

She stopped abruptly, and gasped.

Ahead of her stretched a street she'd seen in countless musicals. Impulsively, she caught hold of Matt's arm. Horrified at what she'd done without thinking, she released it at once, hoping he hadn't noticed.

'Wow, Mr Hunter! I know this street like the back of my hand. I adore those big musicals of the past—I must've seen them hundreds of times.'

He smiled at her. 'I saw from the agency details that you were a real fan, so I figured you'd appreciate this. They've left the street untouched as a tribute to that era.'

She looked at him in surprise. 'I thought you didn't read my details.'

He shrugged. 'I glanced at them last night. I wanted to see exactly what I'd got myself into.'

'I see.' She turned back to the street. 'Just looking at all the familiar shopfronts and signs, it makes you want to burst out into song, doesn't it?' She ran a few steps forward, opened her arms wide and sang the first two lines of 'There's No Business Like Show Business'.

Then she turned back to him, laughing.

'That's from *Annie Get Your Gun*. It's one of my favourites, too. What about "Ol' Man River"? Where's that come from?' He put his hand across his chest. 'Dat ol' man river...' he sang in an exaggeratedly deep voice.

'Easy,' she exclaimed. '*Show Boat*. How about, "Have Yourself a Merry Little Christmas"?'

'Too simple. It's from *Meet me in St. Louis*. Find something harder.'

'Okay. Try this, then,' she said. '"June is Bustin' Out All Over."'

'That's *Carousel*. They were originally gonna call it *Sobbin' Women*. Can you believe it?'

'That would've been all wrong.'

'I agree. Well, we're almost at the end of the street. So what are we gonna finish on? You choose.'

'Um.' She looked up at the sky. 'Well, the sun's shining and the sky's blue, so there's only one number it can be.' And she started to sing, half-running, half-walking 'Doo-dloo-doo-doo-doo, Doo-dloo-doo-doo-doo-doo ... I'm singing in the rain...'

'... Just singing in the rain,' he joined in, and together they ran along the rest of the street, one on each side of the road, jumping on and off the pavement, singing, 'What a glorious feelin', I'm happy again...'

At the end of the road, they stood and faced each other, laughing too much to finish the song.

He shook his head in wonder. 'Did I just do what I think I did?' he asked, when he was able to speak again.

She nodded. 'Yes, you did. You can blame me for leading you astray.'

'I can't remember when I last did something so completely mad. It's been a real good afternoon, and that was a great way to end it. But end it we must, I'm afraid it's time to get back to the car.'

She wiped her hand across her damp forehead. 'Just as well. It's hot, and I've been running. I must be shining like a beacon.'

'The air conditioning in the car will cool you down.'

'I really enjoyed the day, Mr Hunter. Thank you for showing me around. I'm sure there were plenty of other things you could've been doing.'

'I doubt that any of them would've been half as enjoyable, so I should thank *you*, Miss Carter, for being such good company.'

'You're welcome.' She smiled up at him.

Their eyes met. Both looked quickly away.

'Ah, there's Armando,' Matt said. 'The party's definitely over—it's back to real life now.'

She could take a hint. That afternoon was a one-off. And just as well—working for a dishy boss was going be far easier if she disliked him, and she'd just come perilously close to liking him a lot.

When they reached the limousine, Matt stood aside to let her get in, and then got in beside her. Armando switched on the engine and drove them out of the studio and on to the highway. Leaning back against the plush leather upholstery, Matt stretched out his legs and closed his eyes.

Having arranged the rug over her knees, Leigh stared out of the window, and thought about the day she'd had. Matt wasn't going to be easy to work for, being somewhat given to mood swings, but he was going to be an interesting boss.

When the wind was in the right direction, he could be very pleasant—their day in the studio was proof of that. But when it wasn't, as on her first morning working for him, he could be a real nightmare.

She glanced at the nightmare. His eyes were closed and he was breathing steadily. What amazingly thick long eyelashes for a man, she thought. Then she pulled herself mentally up—she mustn't think like that: the man was her employer.

Dragging her gaze away from his face, she turned her head and stared resolutely through the window at the tree-lined streets they were driving along, forcing herself not to look back at him for the rest of the journey home.

6

———

Van Attwood was outside the house, waiting for them when the car passed between the massive wrought-iron gates and drew up in front of the solid redwood door.

As they got out of the car, Matt turned to Leigh. 'I'd like to do a few letters before dinner—they result from the meeting today. Perhaps you'd come to my study in fifteen minutes.'

'Certainly, Mr Hunter,' she said.

As she followed Matt towards the house, she saw Van greet him with a smile. He widened his smile to include Leigh, and then he took Matt's bag from him, and disappeared with him into the cool interior of the house.

Fifteen minutes later, she knocked at the door to Matt's study, and went inside. He wasn't there. Just as she was about to cross to her chair and wait for him to arrive, the telephone in her office rang.

Dropping her notebook in her haste, she sped across to

her office, flung open the door, ran to her desk and grabbed the phone before it stopped ringing.

It was Fran. Her instinct was to say it was a really bad time and she'd ring her back later, but with Matt not yet in the office, she decided to allow herself a few minutes with Fran, but no more than that.

'Hi, Fran,' she said. 'This'll have to be quick. I'm waiting for Mr Hunter. He's got some things he wants me to do.'

'I couldn't wait any longer for you to call. I want the full low down—every teeny weeny detail, and some of the big ones, too.'

'While it's lovely to hear your voice, Fran, I really can't talk now. I'll have to ring you later.'

'I guess I can wait a bit longer,' Fran said gloomily. 'I probably should've left it till the evening to ring—but I was real curious about how you were getting on. I expect you to tell me every single detail on Saturday.'

'Saturday! What's Saturday?'

'The party Jim and I are giving for Joni, of course. It's her birthday. Don't say you've forgotten. You must come—it wouldn't be the same without you. And everyone's dying to hear what Matt Hunter's like.'

'There's nothing to tell yet. I've only just started.' She hesitated. 'I don't know, Fran. I'd completely forgotten about Joni's birthday. I'd obviously like to come, but I'm not sure if it'd be wise to ask for time off so soon.'

'I'm sure he won't mind.'

'You don't know him! To be honest, I didn't get off to a brilliant start, and to sound as if I'm gagging to go to a party minutes after I started here isn't the image I want to present.'

'Everyone's entitled a day or two off in the week. And we planned this before you knew about the job. I'm certain he'll let you come.'

'I'm not! Oh, all right, then. I promise I'll ask later. But I must go now. I'll call you about Saturday.'

'Do your best, won't you?'

'You can count on it. You know me and parties. Quickly, what time does it begin?'

'My place, at about nine. Don't worry about bringing a bottle—Jim's got in a load of drink. And it's only the few of us.'

'As I say, I'll try. But you've no idea what he's like.'

'Indeed, what *is* he like, Miss Carter?' Matt Hunter's voice came from behind her.

'Gotta go, Fran. Bye!' She put the phone back on the receiver, and turned round.

Matt Hunter's blue eyes pierced her. 'Well?' he prompted.

'My friend rang. How long have you been there?'

'Long enough,' he said. 'That's not exactly an answer to my question, but as I've a suspicion it's all I'm gonna get, perhaps we could do some work now.'

She followed him back into his study, and sat down opposite him.

He must have picked up her notebook as it was on his desk in front of her, she noticed. She had an awful suspicion that he'd virtually followed her into his office, and as she'd left the door to her room wide open, he'd have heard the whole of her conversation.

He leaned forward to begin dictating.

His private telephone rang.

Giving her a glance of apology, he picked up the receiver.

'Yes?' he said. As he listened to the voice at the other end, his expression darkened. Leigh made as if to get up, intending to leave the room and give him some privacy, but he gestured for her to stay where she was, and she sat back down again.

Listening to him, she felt sorry for the person at the other end of the line. Her boss was clearly furious at what he was hearing, and said so loudly and often. Then abruptly he hung up. He was tense and angry, she could see, but he was also upset.

He pushed his hair back from his face in a gesture of frustration.

'Right,' he said, making a visible effort to pull himself together. 'First of all, a letter to Bob Lieberman.'

And he began dictating a letter to the producer at such a speed that she struggled to keep up with him. After that, he started on some business letters.

The phone rang again.

With an exclamation of annoyance, he picked up the receiver. 'You again!' he exclaimed, and he swivelled his leather chair so that its back was facing Leigh.

Perfect timing, she thought in relief, and she relaxed. His dictation had been relentless, and her right hand was quite numb from such rapid note taking. She waved her hand in the air a few times, trying to get some feeling back into it.

Matt seemed to be listening this time, she noticed, rather than talking. It sounded like a woman's voice at the other end, but whoever it was, he clearly wasn't pleased at what was being said.

While she waited for the call to finish, she looked down at her notes. His command of finances was quite impressive. He was clearly a bright man, and not just a very dishy one.

Mentally rapping her knuckles for allowing herself to think in terms of how gorgeous-looking he was, she glanced idly at the items on his desk.

A framed photograph stood next to his clock. The photo

was difficult for her to see from her chair, but Matt would have seen it whenever he checked the time.

Curious, she leaned forward and saw that it was of a young girl of about twelve or thirteen. Despite a brace on her teeth, the girl was very pretty. Her long fair hair hung loosely, and she was beaming into the camera with a wide, infectious smile. That must be Carey, she thought, and she found herself smiling back at the photo.

'Absolutely not!' Matt shouted into the phone. 'It's out of the question.'

He spun his chair violently round to face Leigh. There was an angry tic in his jaw as he glared into the receiver. 'Why? What business is it of yours?' There was a pause while he listened to the reply. 'Well, since you ask, it's because I'm already doing something on Saturday. I'm going to ...' He faltered. 'I'm going to ...' Again he stopped.

Leigh could see him struggling. Feeling quite sorry for him, she leaned forward, manoeuvred herself into his line of vision, pointed to herself and mouthed a willingness to help.

His eyes focused on her, and a slow smile spread across his face. Visibly relaxing, he leaned back in his chair.

'It's because I'm going to a party on Saturday evening,' he said calmly. He threw a sly glance at Leigh. 'It's a prior engagement, by invitation only. And before you ask, no, I can't cancel.'

He put down the phone and smiled sweetly across the desk. 'What time did you say the party was, Miss Carter? I'll need to order the car for us.'

7

'What do you mean—the party?' Leigh's eyes opened wide in shock. 'You're not coming with me, are you?'

Instinctively, she knew the answer.

Matt pulled his leather-bound diary towards him and picked up his pen.

'On the phone just now, you sounded desperate to go to the party,' he said smoothly. 'If I heard correctly, you described the strength of your desire as gagging for it. Extreme desperation can damage mental health. Far be it from me to stand in the way of your sanity, Miss Carter. Now, what's Fran's address?'

'That doesn't mean you have to come!' She felt herself going red.

'What an unusual working relationship, we have,' he murmured. 'I, the boss, say what will be, and you, the employee, challenge it. How novel.'

'You'd hate it. It's not a proper party. It's just a few of us getting together for Joni's birthday, with a bit of food and some cheap wine. You'd be dead bored.'

'It sounds quite delightful—you've convinced me.' He paused, drumming his pen on the desk. 'But maybe there's a problem with me coming?' An ominous note flickered in the depths of his eyes.

'Well, not if you really want to,' she said gloomily.

Some party this was going to be! With Matt Hunter there, her friends wouldn't be able to have a good laugh like they always did, and she'd be worrying the whole time about him being bored. She groaned aloud.

'Did you say something?'

'I was clearing my throat.'

'That's good. It means you'll be able to give me Fran's address with clarity of voice.'

Beaten, she told him where Fran lived.

'One other thing, Miss Carter,' he added, when she'd finished. 'Should I wear a posh frock?'

A picture of Matt Hunter in a dress sprang instantly to her mind, and she burst out laughing.

He started to laugh with her.

Her heart gave a sudden lurch. The smile had lit up his face, and the laughter lines crinkling in the corner of his eyes radiated warmth. He really was very fanciable. If he remained silent.

She shook herself. Thinking like that was a huge no-no.

'I wouldn't advise it,' she said shakily, her voice sounding strange in her ears. 'We're really informal.'

'Why's that not a surprise?' He closed the diary. 'I know we've only done a few letters, but we've covered Bob's, which was the most important one, and I'm no longer in the mood to do any more so we'll leave the others till the morning. You can go now.'

As she stood up, he pulled what looked like a script from the pile of papers in front of him, and opened it.

'Oh, just one other thing, Miss Carter,' he called as she went across to the door. 'Matt comes before Hunter. Use it, and I'll feel free to call you Leigh. After all, we *are* going out together on Saturday night, aren't we?'

The clear blue eyes that looked at Leigh were open wide in innocence.

Clutching her notebook tightly, she opened the door and pulled it shut behind her.

It didn't completely close, and as she started walking away, she heard Matt say into the intercom, 'I reckon you meant well, Van, but don't ever put Cybill through to me again. Anything she wants to say to me, she can write. If she phones, you deal with it. I hope that's clear. And one other thing, you can put in your diary that I'll be out on Saturday evening—I'm going to some party or other with Miss Carter.'

VAN SAT BACK in his office and stared at the intercom. His eyes narrowed.

So Matt was going to a party with Leigh Carter, was he? It showed that he'd been right about her all along—like every other tramp that crossed his path, she'd had her sights set on golden boy from the outset.

But unlike with all of the others, his every sense was telling him that she seemed to be getting somewhere with Matt, and quickly, too.

Informal though Matt might be, in the past he'd always kept his distance from the people he met, whether he met them socially or on a work basis. He'd known instinctively where to draw the line. This time, however, the lines seem to have blurred.

Leigh Carter was a pretty girl, it was true, but LA was full of pretty girls, so it was more than likely only the novelty of her lack of sophistication, which might well be an act, that was diverting Matt.

But whatever it was, if he didn't do something soon, before long the Carter feet might be under the table.

And Cybill wouldn't like that. Not at all.

She was going to be spitting mad when she heard that her ex was getting close to a nobody from England.

The last thing Cybill would want to see was her ex find personal happiness in addition to all of the other good things that had landed in his lap.

He glanced at the telephone on his desk. The temptation to contact her and bring her up-to-date was overwhelming, but there was a risk, albeit a faint one, that someone might overhear him, and no one must know that he'd kept in touch with Cybill since her divorce from Matt. He'd have to be patient.

And patient he could be.

He'd had years in which to master the art; years in which he'd seen his dreams turn to dust and his self-respect sink into the mire of servitude; years in which he'd been forced to watch helplessly while someone less talented than he had become the toast of Hollywood and beyond.

Well, helpless he may have been during those years, but helpless he was no longer.

Cybill was using him for sure, but *he* would be using *her*.

She erroneously thought that they were both working for the same goal—to get Cybill back on the A list, and to see him being given a part worthy of his talent, which would put him firmly on the road to success.

But he had a goal that transcended those, a very pressing goal.

One way or another, he was going to exact his revenge

on Leigh Carter and Matt Hunter for the humiliation he'd suffered at their hands.

Everything else paled into insignificance in the face of that.

8

———

From her very first day in the house, Leigh had felt at home with Conchita Perez, Matt Hunter's cook and housekeeper, who'd done everything she could to help Leigh settle.

Every morning, Conchita started Leigh's day with a cup of steaming coffee, which she brought to her on the veranda outside Leigh's office, the delicate scent of dew-encrusted jasmine mingling with the powerful aroma of the coffee.

Conchita's leathery face was creased with laughter lines, and her glossy black hair was swept into a bun that hung loosely at the nape of her neck. Whatever the time of day, she wore a large apron pulled around her ample figure.

She and her husband, Armando, had looked after Matt Hunter for years. Armando, always smiling, oversaw the garden and was Matt Hunter's chauffeur. Even though he'd been in Los Angeles for years, his knowledge of English was fairly poor, and his speech heavily accented.

Their daughter, Maria, was a lively twelve-year-old, a miniature of her mother.

Maria had got on brilliantly with Matt Hunter's daughter, Carey, in the days when Carey used to stay regularly with her father, Conchita had told Leigh. But that had been some time ago, and both Maria and Conchita very much missed Carey's visits.

As she sat in the kitchen with a glass of homemade lemonade on the Saturday morning, she remarked to Conchita that she couldn't believe how fast the week had gone.

'In a few hours it'll be Joni's party,' she said. 'I can't wait to see Fran again.'

'It go fast because we very busy, Miss Leigh.'

'I'm not in the way, am I, sitting here like this?'

'You fine,' Conchita said. 'I making tacos. You have for lunch. Maybe you not eat enough tonight.'

Conchita paused in the middle of mixing salsa into minced beef, and looked across at Leigh. 'Mr Matt go with you tonight. That very nice,' she said, and then she returned her attention to the bowl and continued stirring the mixture, a slight smile on her lips.

'I know what you're getting at, Conchita,' Leigh said, laughing. 'And you couldn't be more wrong. Matt's using me as an excuse not to do something he doesn't want to do. As far as I'm concerned, I can't wait for tonight to be over.'

'You funny girl, Miss Leigh,' Conchita said beaming at her, and she went across to the fridge and took out a bowl of refried beans. 'Mr Matt work too much. It good he go out. He have Van as friend, and many people. But I think he lonely man.'

'Why did Carey stop coming?'

'Miz Harding stop her. We all very sad. Mr Matt very sad, too. He still very sad.'

'It does sound very hard on him, and on Carey,' Leigh

said. She finished her lemonade, sat for a few minutes, and then stood up.

'You know, I think I might go for a swim a bit later. Matt won't be using the pool as he's out, and Van's out, too. I'll finish the mail, have lunch and then have a quick dip in the water, and maybe a few minutes in the sun. After that, I'll trawl through the closet, decide what to wear tonight, and get ready. I probably won't see you till breakfast tomorrow.'

WITH LONG LEISURELY STROKES, Leigh covered the length of the pool and back, and then quickened her pace for the next two lengths. A final length of breast stroke brought her back to the wide stone steps that were close to the lounger where she'd left her robe and sun cream, and she climbed out of the pool and went across for her towel.

The sun beat down on her as she began to towel-dry the worst of the damp from her hair.

It had been a great idea to go swimming, she thought, rubbing her head hard—she now felt much more alive, and better able to cope with the awkwardness of going to the party with her boss.

Heaven knows what Fran was going to say when she rolled up with him!

She hadn't warned Fran that he might come as there was always an outside chance—an outside hope, rather—that when it came to it, he'd think it as ghastly an idea as she thought it, and would pull out.

If only he would.

She threw the towel on the lounger, adjusted the parasol to prevent the sun from falling directly on to her, lay back on the lounger, and pictured herself arriving alone at Fran's, able to let her hair down and go mad with her friends, free from inhibitions caused by anyone or anything.

Bliss.

Closing her eyes, she started drifting off.

FRANTICALLY, she stared at the clothes in her closet—she still hadn't a clue what to wear, having changed her mind every day since the plan was made, and now, at the eleventh hour, she was left with insufficient time in which to decide.

If only she hadn't been so relaxed by the pool that she'd fallen into a deep sleep that had gone on for much too long.

Her gaze ran swiftly along the rails in the hope that something would leap out at her. She and her friends weren't into getting dressed up, and they certainly weren't into high fashion, which she assumed was the style that Matt was used to, given the circles he moved in. He dated sleek, sophisticated girls, Tom had said. Well, there was nothing in her closet that came even close to that!

It was a party, though, so she needed something partyish.

But it mustn't show too much flesh as she'd be there with her boss. And the skirt mustn't be too tight. That horrendous first morning in the car with Matt, when her skirt had stubbornly refused to cover her thighs, was the stuff of nightmares, and she wasn't about to risk a repeat performance.

In the end, she settled for her favourite sage green dress, took it from its hanger, stepped into it, pulled up the shoe-string straps and glanced in the mirror. It would do. The green of the dress set off her auburn curls, and as she had a light tan, all she needed was a trace of lip-gloss, and she was ready to go.

She looked nervous, but that wasn't exactly surprising—she was dreading the evening ahead. But at the same time, if she was truly honest with herself, a part of her was quite excited.

However it had come about, unless he pulled out at the last minute, she was about to spend several hours in the company of a man who could be charming when he wanted, and fun to be with, and who was quite the most attractive man she'd ever met.

Yes, there was most definitely something within her that was looking forward to the party, despite her gnawing anxiety about what Matt would make of her friends.

Well, here goes, she thought. She applied her lip-gloss, slipped into her sage green heels, picked up her small green-beaded bag and went out to meet her companion for the evening.

MATT WAS LEANING against a sleek black Mercedes SL convertible. The top was down and Armando was nowhere to be seen.

As she walked up to him, she felt his eyes on her, and she shivered.

'Perhaps you should have worn something warmer,' he murmured as he opened the passenger door and stepped aside for her to enter the car.

'I'm sure you'll be a source of sufficient hot air,' she retorted without thinking. She pulled a face. 'Gosh, I'm sorry,' she said. 'I shouldn't have said that—it was rude of me.'

'Think nothing of it,' he replied smoothly. 'I'm getting quite used to the unusual nature of your responses. In fact, there's a certain excitement in not knowing what you'll come out with next.'

He closed the passenger door behind her, went round to the driver's side of the car, slid in and fastened his seat belt.

'Is it okay with you if we leave the top down?' he asked.

'Definitely. It's a lovely evening.'

'I'm sure it will be.' He turned to the road, switched on the engine and guided the car through the gates.

'I was talking about the weather,' she remarked, as he negotiated the winding roads.

'I know.'

Leaving behind them the lavish mansions of Bel Air, all of which stood back from the road in carefully manicured gardens bordered by glossy green foliage, the world kept at bay by walls and wrought-iron gates, they drove out on to the broad sweep of Santa Monica Boulevard. Matt swung the wheel sharply and the car roared off in the direction of Brentwood.

As she leaned back against the leather headrest, enjoying the feel of the wind in her hair, she sneaked a sideways look at him.

He was wearing stone-coloured chinos and a shirt of the same colour, open at the neck, its sleeves rolled back to his elbows, in the way that he always liked. His dark brown leather belt was clasped in a heavy buckle. The phrase drop-dead gorgeous sprang into her mind.

One of his arms rested carelessly on the side of the convertible, and with the other, he skilfully controlled the car. Her eyes were drawn to the hand that was guiding the steering wheel with consummate ease. He tightened his grip on the wheel, and the muscles in his arm flexed.

She felt a sudden overwhelming urge to reach out and

run the palm of her hand slowly down the length of his arm, to feel his hard muscle beneath her fingertips.

She mentally recoiled. What was she thinking of, she thought in horror, and she stared back at the road, aghast.

'Are you all right, Leigh?' she heard him ask, a note of concern in his voice. 'You look a little flushed. There's not too much air on your face, is there? I'll put the top up, if you like.'

'No, thank you. I'm fine. I love the wind in my face.' At that moment, anything that could cool her down was at the top of her wish-for list!

'A dime for your thoughts,' he said a few minutes later, as they waited at the traffic lights. 'You've gone unusually quiet.'

'I was wondering what you'll make of Fran's place,' she lied. She could hardly tell her boss that it was taking every bit of concentration to keep her eyes on the road and not on him. 'It's really unusual,' she added for extra authenticity.

'In what way?'

'She can't resist interesting objects, and her house is full of Native American and Aztec artefacts, as well as her own pottery.'

'Does she sell her things?'

'When she can. She used to teach pottery evening classes in Brentwood, which is where I met her. We hit it off at once: we've got the same sense of humour...'

'Now that *is* a scary thought!' The lights turned green and he started the car again.

'... and we became good friends,' she went on, deciding not to rise to his comment. 'I stopped the classes a while ago, but we stayed friends.'

'She sounds a character.'

'She certainly is, Mr Hunter; as you will see.'

'It's Matt. Remember? You can't call your date for the evening anything that begins with a mister.'

'I'll skip over your misuse of the word date as there's something I wanted to ask you,' she said awkwardly.

'That sounds serious,' he said cheerfully. 'Ask away, but I might plead the Fifth.'

'Feel free to incriminate yourself—I promise not to tell anyone.' She cleared her throat. 'When you decided to come tonight, you wanted an excuse to avoid meeting someone—'

'Yup, my ex-wife.'

'Why not just say you were going to a private party, but not go to the party? She'd never have known if you stayed at home or went somewhere else. So why *did* you come?'

There was a pause. His eyes were fixed on the road ahead.

'I don't really know,' he said after a moment or two. 'I asked myself the same question this afternoon, and I couldn't come up with a good answer. I guess I thought your party might pass the evening quite pleasantly.'

'But I said it'd be deadly dull, with wine that was almost undrinkable!'

He shrugged. 'It was something different, and I thought it might be fun. Being with movie folk isn't necessarily fun—glamorous maybe, but not fun. They're a narcissistic bunch, and envious and watchful of each other, which isn't the most relaxing thing. I can't remember when I last went to a party that had nothing to do with films or business, and I think I was rather drawn to the idea.' He glanced at her. 'I'm afraid that's the best I can do.'

'I suppose it's a pretty good best,' she said reluctantly. 'I only hope your civvie night out lives up to your expecta-tions,' she added lightly, watching the UCLA buildings flash by.

They were now only minutes away from Fran's, she realised, and excitement welled up in her at the thought of seeing her friends again.

'That's the house,' she cried as they rounded a corner. 'You can park in front.'

The door was flung open as Matt drew up at the kerb, and a woman in an ankle-length deep red silk caftan with a *lei* of brightly coloured flowers swinging around her neck, came running down the steps.

'Fran!' Leigh exclaimed. She jumped out of the car, ran to her friend and hugged her. 'You're still in your Hawaiian phase, I see,' she said laughing as she pulled back to look at her, and she hugged her again.

'We're so pleased you could make it. So the old—' Fran stopped abruptly and stared over Leigh's shoulder.

Leigh felt her friend go rigid.

Then she remembered Matt Hunter behind her, and quickly stood back from Fran, and turned towards Matt to introduce them to each other.

But Matt had moved forward. 'Do finish your sentence, Fran—it *is* Fran, isn't it?' he said, holding out his hand. 'What comes after the old?'

Leigh stepped quickly in.

'Fran, this is my employer, Matt Hunter. He wanted to join us. I hope that's okay. I didn't tell you he was coming because I thought he might drop out at the last moment. Matt, you're right—this is my friend, Fran.'

Matt shook Fran's hand.

'I'm delighted to meet you,' he said warmly. 'As a small apology for arriving uninvited, I'd like to contribute to the wine for the evening, if I may.' He moved to the back of the car and took a container with several bottles of wine from the boot.

'No contribution's necessary. You're welcome to join us,' Fran murmured, throwing Leigh a look that mixed amazement with curiosity.

But Matt was already carrying the wine up the steps to the house. In his other hand, he held a long, narrow box.

'So it's Matt now, is it?' Fran whispered to Leigh as they followed him. 'He seems nice.'

'He's Matt to everyone who works for him,' Leigh retorted, 'so don't read anything into that. As for being nice, he's a bit of a mixture.'

'I can't wait to hear everything. Obviously not now—too many people around—but later when we can sneak off.'

A loud scream sounded from inside the house.

Following the sound, they hurried past strings of brightly coloured gourds to the den. There they found Joni in the middle of the room, shrieking with delight as she gazed at the perfect white orchid that had been presented to her by the uninvited guest.

'That is so kind,' she cried, smiling radiantly up at Matt. 'Thank you, thank you.' She turned to Leigh. 'And thank you, Leigh, for bringing this lovely man with you.'

Leigh cringed.

Shut up, Joni, she urged inwardly, and she looked desperately around to see how she could drag Matt Hunter away from Joni.

She liked Joni enormously, but Joni could gush for America and was renowned for saying the wrong thing at the wrong time. Which, Leigh realised, horrified, Joni was already starting to do.

'And what do you think of our little English friend?' Joni asked Matt.

'Must I answer that?' he murmured.

'Isn't she absolutely the best secretary you've ever had?' she trilled.

Leigh prayed that the earth would swallow her up. And Joni, too.

'She's certainly the most interesting one,' he said dryly. He glanced at Leigh, a smile of malicious amusement hovering around his lips.

'Yes, she's so interesting, isn't she? You are so right. And she's real entertaining, too,' bubbled Joni.

Did California still have the death penalty, Leigh wondered.

Matt's raised eyebrow was encouragement enough for Joni to continue.

'Don't you remember, Leigh, how you forgot to note where you'd parked the car when we went to Disneyland and it took us five hours to find it, the car park is so huge?'

'Hysterical,' Matt said, his voice lost in a slight cough.

Joni was making her sound like a total idiot, she thought, appalled. If she could just get hold of the birthday orchid, she'd smother Joni with it!

'And Leigh's car—well, station wagon really. It was such a character.' Joni was unstoppable. 'You called her Griselda, didn't you, Leigh?'

Now she was someone who gave a name to her car! Not an American custom, but a British one. Try telling that to Matt Hunter, though. He must think he'd hired a nutcase.

She tried to flash a warning to Joni, but the birthday girl was oblivious.

Inspiration struck! 'Fran, why don't you take Matt to meet Jim?' Leigh asked, her voice strained.

But at that moment, Fran's partner, Jim, materialised, found out what Matt was drinking and soon had a glass in his hand. They fell into conversation, and Joni moved off to check on her husband.

Leigh heaved a huge sigh of relief.

Turning down the offer of wine as she didn't want to risk making even more of a fool of herself than Joni had managed to make of her, she started moving around the room and chatting to her friends.

They were all eager to hear the low-down about life in Matt's household, but she fended them off with a joke—she wasn't about to pass on details about his private life.

Every so often she sneaked a glance at Matt, just to make sure he was having a good time.

To her relief, her friends seemed relaxed around him and conversation appeared to be flowing. They were all laughing a lot, including Matt, and from the snatches of conversation that reached her, she could tell they were talking about normal things—films, restaurants, the endless traffic jams, the best coffee to buy. If he wasn't enjoying their company, no one would ever have known.

Once or twice she thought she'd felt his eyes on her, but when she'd turned quickly towards him, he'd been looking elsewhere each time.

Gradually a heaviness crept over her. She realised that the strain of starting a new job, and a live-in one at that, had chosen the worst possible time to catch up with her, and despite her sleep in the afternoon, she felt a weight of fatigue pressing upon her.

Deciding that the best thing to do was to have a very short rest, and then throw herself properly into the party, she took herself off to Fran's sitting room and sank into the large sofa.

Sounds coming from the kitchen and beyond told her that Fran was setting out a buffet on the patio, but it was too much effort to go for food and she leaned back, closed her eyes and gave herself up to sleep.

In what seemed a matter of moments, a rush of air was washing over her, followed by the sofa sinking and rising. She opened her eyes. Matt had sat down next to her and was holding out a plate on which Fran's chicken *luau* was piled high next to a heap of fried rice and a slab of corn bread.

'I'm not hungry,' she said, 'which must be a first. But thank you, anyway.'

'Try some. It's delicious. Fran said it's your favourite.' He pushed the plate into one hand, and a fork into the other.

It took one mouthful only for Leigh to realise she was ravenous, and she ate until her plate was empty.

'What about a drink?' Matt asked, taking the empty plate from her and standing up.

'Just a glass of water, please—I'm avoiding wine this evening. I hadn't realised how hungry I was. Thanks for spotting it.'

He grinned at her. 'Your appetite is legendary.'

She gave a theatrical groan. 'How flattering to be known as a garbage can.'

'Don't knock it. You look pretty good on it.'

She stared up at him in surprise.

The deep blue eyes that looked back at her were filled with something that looked suspiciously like warmth.

Neither of them moved.

Then abruptly he turned and went out into the hall, passing Fran, who was hovering in the doorway.

'Look at the two of you!' Fran exclaimed, hurrying into the room. 'You look great together. He's a real neat guy, Leigh.'

'Don't make it into what it isn't,' Leigh interrupted. 'I

admit he was being kind and saying nice things, but it'll have been the drink talking. That's all.'

'Only you and Matt know if you've clicked,' Fran said. 'But you're wrong about one thing: Matt's had one glass only —he's the second most sober person here.'

She finished speaking just as the second most sober person returned.

'When you've drunk this, we should leave,' he said, handing Leigh a glass of water. 'You look exhausted.'

She took the glass from him. 'Blame it on that slave-driver boss of mine.'

They smiled at each other.

Fran gave a short cough.

MATT STOOD ASIDE to let Leigh enter the house ahead of him.

He closed the door behind them. 'I've never known you so quiet. You've not said a single word since we left Fran's.'

'I was thinking about things.'

'I hope you were thinking that you enjoyed the evening, because I was.'

She looked up at him. 'Were you really, Matt? You looked as if you were having fun. But then you would— you're an actor.'

'I had a terrific time. If I hadn't been enjoying myself, we'd have left a long time before we did. I envy you your friends, Leigh—they're a great bunch. It's hard in my job to make true friends as I never know if it's me they like or the trappings of success.'

She nodded. 'I can see how difficult it must be.'

'But fortunately, I've got Van as a friend. We go way back,

and I'm real relieved that the luck I've had over the years has never got in the way of our friendship.'

'I'm so relieved you had a good time—I thought you might be bored.'

'Not at all. In fact, I haven't had a boring moment since you started working for me.' He frowned slightly. 'Actually, that's true, you know. I hadn't realised it till now.' He gave an awkward laugh.

'Anyway, thank you for helping to make it such a lovely evening for my friends.'

'I'm not sure you should be thanking me—I barged into something that was for you and your friends, ignoring the fact that you clearly didn't want me there. I'm sorry for that, but I'm glad I did it.'

'Me, too,' she said.

'I wonder if you really are.' A half-smile on his lips, his eyes slowly traced her face.

For a wild moment, she wondered if he was going to kiss her, and her heart missed a beat.

But with a slight wave of his hand, he turned and went along the corridor towards his wing.

She stood and watched him until he was completely out of sight.

As if he would kiss someone like her, she thought in a moment of sudden despair. She must've lost her senses. And she turned and made her way back to her room.

9

The scent of the white jasmine growing up the wall outside her office and around the glass doors drifted towards Leigh as she stared towards the pool. The water glistened invitingly beneath the strong rays of the late morning sun, and the thought of a swim was increasingly tempting.

It was Sunday, and she had the day to herself and could go for a swim if she wanted. But she didn't know what Matt was doing, beyond the fact he was at home, and, with it being a hot day, he might well decide to head for the pool himself.

And no way she'd want to be in the water, clad in the one-and-only swimsuit she'd brought with her—a minis-cule yellow bikini—when he rolled up poolside! That would be the ultimate in embarrassment.

The only way to make sure of that not happening was to keep well away from the water, so that's what she would do.

She turned, went into the cool of her office, and sat down behind her desk. She'd got some letters to answer on

Matt's behalf, and she'd get on with that, rather than leave them for the following day.

She took the cover off her typewriter and pulled the first of the letters towards her. There was a light tap on her door, and she paused. Before she could call 'Come in', the door opened and Van entered her office, a large file in his hand.

'Surely you're not working on your day off, Leigh?'

'It's not that easy to take time off when you live and work in the same place. There's always something you could be doing work-wise.'

'How very true. And as you'll see, I'm no different,' he said with a smile, and he indicated the file in his hand. 'I've brought copies of the documents I'm taking to the accountants tomorrow. I thought to leave them for you to file when you've a moment.'

'No problem. Just put them down and I'll do them later. I'll probably work through the afternoon.'

He placed the file on her desk, and stood hovering next to her. She looked up at him questioningly.

'I believe you and Matt went to a party last night,' he said. 'I trust you had a successful evening.'

'I don't know about successful, but it was extremely pleasant. I'd been worried that Matt would be bored as although my friends are really nice, they're very ordinary. But they all seemed to get on well together and he appeared to enjoy himself.'

'I'm glad to hear it. He doesn't relax enough. I'm always telling him he should go out socially more often. Perhaps you'll go out somewhere else together before too long.'

She flushed. 'It wasn't going out together, as such—Matt just came along. I very much doubt we'll be doing anything like that again.'

* * *

VAN'S LIPS were compressed in a thin line as he headed for his office.

Leigh Carter was right—successful wasn't the correct word.

She hadn't quite succeeded in her ultimate goal since she'd clearly spent the last night in her own room. But she'd be confident that yesterday's little shindig had put her well on the road to success, even though she'd yet to reach her destination.

Her plans for Matt Hunter were bound to be far more ambitious than having him hang out with a bunch of her loser friends, and no matter what she'd said, she'd already be working on how to engineer another evening out with him, ideally an evening alone with the prize so that she could truly dig her claws into him.

Of that he was certain.

But she'd soon find out that things wouldn't be running quite as smoothly in the future as she'd hoped, he thought in cold satisfaction. On the contrary.

He'd been waiting for the right moment to come along that offered him the chance of avenging himself on them both, and his every instinct told him that, thanks to his intervention, he wasn't going to have to wait for much longer.

And that was a real good feeling.

When he'd contacted Cybill earlier and had run past her an idea that had occurred to him, she'd instantly agreed to do as he'd suggested. At that moment, the wheels of his revenge had been set in motion.

It had been an immense personal satisfaction to hear her fall so readily in with his wishes, but it hadn't been a surprise.

For years he'd worked hard at keeping alive a friendship

with that tiresome, self-absorbed prima donna, feeling instinctively that it was through Cybill Harding that one day he'd be able to strike at Matt Hunter with greatest effect, with the result that Cybill now thought as he wanted her to think.

And Matt Hunter believed that he, Matt Hunter, was a great actor. Well, he should have watched Van over the past few years! He might have learnt a thing or two.

Like everyone else, Matt had underestimated Van's talent for acting. He didn't have a fraction of the talent that he, Van, had in his little finger, and his success over the years with both Matt and Cybill was proof of that.

When he reached his office door, he paused for a moment. If all went according to plan, Matt Hunter would soon be blasted out of his smug complacency, and Leigh Carter would be out in the cold, her hopes for success with Matt Hunter torn into little shreds.

A smile of quiet satisfaction twisting his lips, he pushed the door open, went inside and closed the door firmly behind him.

LEIGH WOKE with a jolt as the sound of splashing water broke into the quiet of the afternoon.

Rubbing her eyes, she glanced over the side of the lounger and saw that her book had slipped from her stomach and was on the ground. So much for her plan to spend the afternoon reading.

After working all morning on Matt's correspondence, and then filing the documents Van had given her, she'd decided to call it a day work-wise, and to give herself a break on what promised to be a very hot afternoon.

She'd had lunch with Conchita in the kitchen, slipped

into a yellow sundress, and had then settled down on the lounger in front of her office.

She remembered kicking off her strappy yellow sandals, stretching out on the lounger and opening her book, but nothing after that.

The sound of someone in the pool must have woken her up.

Curious, she sat upright and stared in the direction of the water, but she was too low down to see above the abundant bushes and shrubs that were in the way. So she stood up, slipped into her sandals and moved to the edge of the terrace where she had an unobstructed view.

It was Matt. He was swimming lengths, devouring the pool with long, powerful strokes and an easy grace.

Mesmerised by his motion, she leaned against one of the veranda posts, and squinting against the glare of the sun, watched him.

Finally, he coasted to the side and hauled himself effortlessly on to the paved surround where he stood, his broad shoulders and strong legs glistening and golden beneath the sparkling droplets of water that coursed to the ground.

She caught her breath. *He really is beautiful*, she breathed inwardly.

Her gaze followed him as he strolled across to a sun lounger, picked up his towel, rubbed it briefly over his body, and then put on his white towelling robe and walked across to the cabana.

'Damn!' she exclaimed out loud in disappointment as he went into the building and out of sight, and she decided to stay in position and wait for him to appear again.

To her great annoyance, her office phone rang.

Furious at whoever was at the other end of the line, she ran inside and snatched up the receiver.

'Yes,' she snapped.

'You're not much use to me over there, Leigh. But you could be of some use to me over here. So come and be of some use.'

The line went dead.

Why, oh, why, had she been so silly as to stand and watch him, she wailed. If she'd given it a moment's thought, she'd have realised that he might see her.

If only she'd stayed on the lounger, she'd have been hidden from sight and he'd never have known she was there. But now that he did, she'd have to do as he asked.

She picked up her notebook and pen, figuring that he'd probably want to dictate some notes, gave a loud sigh, left the office and hurried towards the pool, her sandals clattering noisily on the paving stones that led across the lawn.

He was sitting on the side of the lounger, facing her direction, looking down at what appeared to be a script. As she drew near, he glanced up and rose to his feet.

Her steps faltered.

His robe hung open, revealing a hard chest. A suggestion of muscle rippled beneath its bronzed surface. A light covering of rough chest hair tapered down to his low-slung trunks.

Her eyes followed the line of his chest hair to the waistband of his trunks, and her mouth felt dry.

Dragging her eyes away from his body, she saw that it *had* been a script he'd been reading, and he'd been making notes in the margin.

She licked her lips nervously. 'What would you like me to do?'

He tapped the sheets. 'Read through some of these lines with me. I know it's your day off, and if you want to say no, that's fine. But if you've got a bit of time, though, and don't mind helping, I'd be real grateful. I'm blocking the lines, and it's easier to do that with two people.'

She shrugged her shoulders. 'If you want, I will. But I can't act.'

'It's not an audition. All I want you to do is read.'

'How many parts do you want me to read?'

'Just one. It's a scene for two people. I'll read the other. It'll help me get a feel for movement, expression, and so on. You know the sort of thing. You must have helped producers in the past.'

'Not like this I haven't.' She hesitated. She felt suspicious, but she wasn't sure what she was suspicious about. 'I thought you rehearsed a scene before you filmed it, so why d'you need to read it through now?' she asked.

He dropped the script on the lounger, pulled the towelling belt round him and did it up.

'Time's money,' he said. He sat down and picked up the script again, 'so rehearsal time is short. I always prefer to have a clear idea of what I'm doing before we rehearse it on the set. If you don't want to, you don't have to. It's up to you. But if you *do* decide to give me a hand, for heaven's sake take a seat—you're making me nervous.' Impatiently, he indicated the place next to him on his lounger.

She was making *him* nervous!

He fixed his eyes on the script. She noticed that his hair was still damp and water occasionally trickled into the neck of his robe.

'What sort of scene is it?' she asked, crossing to the lounger opposite his and perching on the edge, facing him.

'A scene for two people.'

'I got that much. Are they quarrelling or what?'

He further tightened the belt of his robe, and she thought she saw the hint of a blush beneath his tan. 'It's a love scene,' he said, avoiding her eyes. 'But we don't act it out or anything. It's just about the words.'

Her insides did a complete somersault.

She slid further back on to her lounger and focused her attention on her pen.

'Shall we start then?' he asked.

She nodded.

There was a long silence.

'I've only got one copy of the script, Leigh,' he said finally.

'So?' she squeaked.

'So that was why I asked you to sit next to me,' he said with exaggerated patience. 'Are you going to move, or is reading the script upside down from afar one of those superior skills you mentioned?'

Glaring at him, she got up and went and sat next to him. He held the script between them so that both could read it.

'Let's begin,' he said. 'I'm Charlie, an itinerant worker. I've fallen for the wife of the rancher who owns the farm where I'm working. Her name's Ginnie. Guess what? That's your part.' He gave her an encouraging smile.

'Is Ginnie keen on you?' she asked.

Stupid question, she thought. Who wouldn't be—unless, of course, they were his secretary!

'Yup, but she doesn't want to face it.'

'What bit are we going to read?'

'Things are coming to a head. Ginnie's poured Charlie a beer. He's drinking it slowly, watching her, thinking about making a move on her. She's hanging around, and against her better judgment, kinda hoping he'll make a pass. Do you think you've got the picture?'

'It sounds pretty straightforward.'

'It is. We'll start at the bottom of page eleven. They're making small talk while he drinks the beer.'

He began to read, pausing when it was Leigh's turn, and every so often pencilling a comment on the script. She read her lines without expression. Not so with Matt. Whatever his original intention, he couldn't stop himself from acting out the part.

They continued reading for several minutes, and then Matt suddenly stopped.

'It would be easier if you put in just a bit of expression,' he said irritably. 'D'you think you could do that? At the moment I feel like I'm flirting with a lump of stone.'

'How much expression?' she asked warily. 'I've never been anything more demanding than third servant in a school play.'

'Ginnie has the hots for Charlie, but you sound as if you're reading the shopping list. You have to show the audience that you find me—that you find Charlie—attractive.'

'I told you I wasn't an actress.'

'Ouch!' A half smile played across his lips. 'Okay, just do your best.'

They started to read again, and she tried to put a little more emotion into the words, feeling very self-conscious as she did so. She was certain that Matt Hunter was secretly loving every minute of her discomfort, and that wasn't helping.

As they read on, he put more and more expression into the character of Charlie, every so often marking the margin while she was reading her part. She felt herself relaxing a little, so much so that when he was reading a longer speech, she risked glancing ahead at the stage directions.

Charlie was going to put down his beer, she saw, take a step towards Ginnie and kiss her.

Her heart started to race.

She found herself waiting in suspense for the moment, her nerve-endings tingling, wondering how Matt would handle it. And to her great surprise, desperately hoping that Matt *would* handle it.

At last he reached the final line before the kiss. When he'd read it, he mimed putting the beer down on the table, and then he turned towards her. Her eyes met his, and they stared at each other.

The air between them was thick with tension.

She felt hot all over.

'We'd better stop now,' he said abruptly. He threw the script on to the opposite lounger and stood up. 'I'm grateful to you for reading the lines, but it wouldn't be sensible to go any further into the scene, and I think we should call it a day.'

'You're right,' she said, trying to suppress the huge disappointment she shouldn't have felt, but did. She stood up. 'I ought to get back to the house, anyway—I've got things to do.' Hearing the flatness in her voice, she cleared her throat, picked up her notebook and started to hurry away from the lounger.

She could feel his eyes on her back as she walked.

'Leigh,' she heard him call.

She stopped and turned towards him. 'D'you need anything?'

'Yes, to be allowed to change my mind,' he said, his voice reflecting the discomfort on his face.

Her heart jumped. 'About what?'

'I'm thinking that just maybe, on this hot Sunday afternoon, we should say to hell with doing what's sensible, and finish the Charlie and Ginnie scene. Nailing it is real important.' He hesitated. 'D'you think you could you bear to be Ginnie for a little longer? You don't have to.'

'No, I really couldn't,' she said quickly.

'I understand.'

But she knew that she could, and she knew that she wanted to, even though everything inside her was shrieking out that she shouldn't—that it would be a humdinger of a mistake to do so. She ought to go back to the house at once and take a long cold shower.

But she couldn't move.

'I respect your decision, of course, but since you're still here ...' He went up to her, took her notebook and pen from her hands and placed them on the lounger. Then he picked up the script. 'Charlie was about to kiss Ginnie, wasn't he?'

'Was he?' she stammered.

'Yes, he was, I think you'll find. I'll read the last line before the kiss again. We'll imagine that Ginnie starts clearing away the glasses, but Charlie stops her.'

He started to read from the script. When he reached the final word in the line, he let the script float to the ground, and faced her.

Her heart pounding loudly, her eyes remained fixed on her varnished toenails.

'So here's how it's done on a film set,' he said, placing his hand on the back of her neck.

A frisson of electricity ran through her.

'First of all, you must gaze into Charlie's face. Your eyes reveal that you're fearful of what you know is about to happen, but what you desperately want to happen. And then it happens. That's what's in the script, so that's what we'll do.' With his index finger, he tilted her face to look into his. 'Charlie stares into your eyes,' he said quietly. 'And then he kisses you, Ginnie.'

She froze.

He bent his head, and his mouth came close to hers.

Burning desire and an intense longing for him swept through her, ejecting every ounce of common sense out of her body, and she strained towards him, parting her lips.

Their lips touched.

The sound of breaking glass shattered the moment.

They jumped back, startled. He dropped his arm. Breathing heavily, they stared towards the house, and then looked back at each other.

'I wonder who dropped what,' he said when his breathing had steadied. 'But whatever it was, we were saved by the bell, in a manner of speaking, Probably just as well. No, definitely just as well.' He picked up his script. 'We should've left it as it was and I shouldn't have embarked on that scene.'

'So why did you?' she asked, a tremor in her voice.

He gave her a slow, lazy smile, and shrugged. 'I guess, because I wanted to.'

Her stomach swirled wildly. 'Huh!' was all she could manage, and she picked up her things and walked quickly away.

'An interesting response, Leigh,' he called after her. 'You never let me down.'

Speeding up her steps, she headed for the house and her bedroom as the words that Tom had said before he left flooded unbidden into her mind.

Relentlessly, with every step she took, they drummed louder and louder in her head.

Most of the women Matt met made a play for him, Tom had said. They see him as no more than a stepping stone to a career in the movies, or as someone who could fund for them a lifestyle of ease, and move them into the elite social circle of A-listers.

And Matt himself had implied as much.

Well, anyone who'd watched the two of them just now, who'd seen her instant response to him, would have thought that she was just another woman on the make.

Thank goodness they'd stopped when they had!

Even though Matt had initiated the action, when he looked back on it, which she was sure he would've done, he could easily have decided that her initial reluctance to participate was feigned for the sake of appearances. After all, in next to no time she was showing every sign of being an enthusiastic participant.

It wasn't like that, though. In the heat of the moment, she'd responded without thinking. That was all.

But how could he know that she wasn't after anything from him, that it was just that she found him absolutely gorgeous and great fun to be with and kissing him, given his invitation, had been a natural human response?

He couldn't. He didn't know her.

She put her hands to her head—she couldn't bear the idea of him thinking badly of her. She must never again let herself get into such a situation. From that moment on, her relationship with Matt must be strictly a boss-and-secretary one.

She fell back on her bed, and stared up at the ceiling in misery.

And indeed, that's all they were, a boss and his secretary. So why did she feel so intensely depressed, she wondered.

STANDING on the terrace outside Matt's study, Van stared down at the shards of broken glass that littered the ground.

It was a pity he'd had to sacrifice the crystal decanter in the way that he had, but there'd been no time to find an alternative.

He'd had one moment only in which to make sure that the scene about to be acted out at the side of the pool didn't reach the conclusion written in the script.

And he'd succeeded.

Turning, he walked steadily into the house to arrange for the fragments of glass to be swept up.

10

To Leigh's enormous relief, Matt didn't mention the poolside scene when she reported for work the following morning. In business mode, he'd gestured to her to sit in her usual place, pulled a pile of letters in front of him, and started to dictate the replies.

Just as if there hadn't been that moment of closeness between them the day before.

Thank goodness for that, she thought as she took down his words.

She'd tossed and turned throughout the night, longing for oblivion but unable to sleep, wondering how she could have been stupid enough to have come as close to responding to Matt as she had.

Hour after hour, his face had loomed large in her mind. No matter how closely she'd clutched the pillow to her chest, and rolled over on to a cool patch of sheet in an effort to banish him from her thoughts, still she'd been able to see him, still she'd been able to feel the warmth in his eyes as he'd gazed down on her face.

What could she have been thinking about—he was her boss!

She should've walked away the minute she'd realised he intended to act out the scene. In fact, she should have left even before that. It had been a mad idea for her to read through the scene with him in the first place. He could easily have called in someone else to do that.

Even Van Attwood could've read the lines. And probably better than she'd read them. In Shakespeare's time all the women's parts were played by men, so Matt hadn't really needed to involve her at all.

Why, oh, why had she agreed, she agonised, and she'd rolled over on to her other side.

When morning had finally come, she'd lain in bed, staring at the ceiling, wondering how on earth she was going to get through the day ahead, and dreading facing her boss again. Jumping on the first plane for London, clutching an empty purse, had suddenly seemed amazingly tempting.

Thanks to the burst of energy given her by Conchita's breakfast of hot buttery cinnamon roll and a mug of steaming coffee, she managed to get to her office on time, and even to be ready with the daily listings when Matt buzzed through to her.

But she needn't have worried what he would say when she saw him—he looked distracted and tired, and was clearly no keener on bringing up what had almost happened between them than she.

He'd thrown her a short, searching look, opened his mouth as if to say something, closed it, and had promptly started to dictate a response to the letter on the top of the pile in front of him.

From time to time, when he paused in his dictation, she glanced up from her notebook. Each time, she caught him watching her, and each time he instantly looked away and resumed dictating.

When he finished the letters, he picked up the phone.

'I've got a call to make,' he told her.

On that clear note of dismissal, she went through to her office and began to type up his replies, confident that if she threw herself into her work, she wouldn't have time to think of anything else.

But she was wrong. He was in the back of her mind with every word she typed.

As she was almost at the end of dealing with the replies, her door flew open and Matt came in.

She looked up. 'I'm afraid I've not quite finished.'

'You can finish them later. I'm gonna have a quick word with Van, and then I'm going out. Or rather, *we're* going out. There's a meeting at the studio this afternoon and I want you to take notes. We'll have lunch at the studio. I'd like to leave in half an hour, if you can manage that.'

'Of course.'

He started to walk out, and then paused.

'Just one thing,' he added, glancing back at her with a wry smile. 'You need not worry. We're leaving Charlie and Ginnie back at the farm.'

THIRTY MINUTES LATER, Leigh found Matt already in the driver's seat. She slid in beside him and fastened her seat belt.

'No Armando today?' she asked after they'd driven in silence for a while.

'Nope. I thought I'd drive. I drive myself whenever I can. It can actually be quite relaxing, even in LA traffic. I stand around for too much of my life, waiting for directors to tell the cameras to roll. When I'm behind the wheel of the car, I'm the one in control of the action.'

'Or inaction,' she murmured as they joined the back of a long line of cars.

'There's an unusual amount of traffic today,' Matt remarked a little later as they crawled bumper to bumper along the road.

To her annoyance, Leigh realised she was beginning to feel quite hungry, which wasn't good as they were still some way from the studio. She should've eaten a bigger breakfast, she scolded herself.

About ten minutes later, Matt suddenly swung the wheel sharply to the left and started driving north.

'Where are we going?' she asked.

'You'll see.'

A little while later, she realised in surprise that they were driving along Sunset Boulevard. Not long after that, Matt pulled up in the parking lot behind a building on the Strip.

He got out of the car, and she did the same.

'Where are we going?' she asked as she followed him round to the front of the building.

He nodded towards the words above the entrance. 'The clue's in the word restaurant,' he said with a smile. 'We're gonna eat here. The traffic will have eased off in an hour. By then, we'll have had our lunch and still be in time for the meeting.'

Ignoring glances of recognition from the customers sitting outside on the front terrace, he led the way through to the cool interior of the restaurant.

'People wanting to be noticed usually sit outside,' he told her. 'They get to see and be seen. I prefer the inside.'

The maître d' showed them to a leather banquette at the side of the restaurant and handed them each a menu.

Matt opened his menu, and then closed it. 'I don't need a menu—I come here a lot so I know what they do. I'm gonna have a hamburger. What about you?'

'The same, please.'

'Hamburger and fries for us both,' he told the waiter, 'followed by your special apple tart. And we'll have some sparkling water. Or would you like wine, Leigh? *I* can't because I'm driving.'

'Not for me either, thank you.'

He asked the waiter to bring the food as quickly as possible, and the waiter disappeared.

Matt settled himself against the rear of the banquette. 'It's unlike you not to take a keen interest in what you're about to eat,' he said, his voice teasing. 'I hope you're not sickening for something.'

'I'm hungry, but I'm not, if you see what I mean.'

'I don't, but it's probably wiser not to ask for an explanation.'

'Good call,' she said, and she helped herself to a bread roll from the basket that the waiter had just put on the table.

'Well then, little English enigma, what are we gonna talk about during lunch? Shall we carry on ignoring yesterday, and discuss the hamburgers and the apple tart for which they're justly famous, or shall we put into words what we're both thinking?'

She stared down at the crisp white napkin on her lap.

'Okay, then. Rather than emulate Trappist monks by sitting in silence, I'll start the ball rolling. I'd like to apologise for what happened yesterday, or rather for what didn't happen, but might have happened.'

She looked up at him, a half-smile hovering on her lips.

'That sounds like the sort of convoluted sentence I'd come up with.'

'God forbid that it's catching! Let me move on fast, then. I guess I got carried away yesterday. You, me, the lovesick Charlie, the Californian sun. We should have stopped when I originally suggested.'

He paused.

'It's your turn now,' he prompted.

She took a deep breath. 'As you say, it was the sun's fault. And also, you're an actor. You obviously didn't feel comfortable stopping mid-scene, and part of you wanted to act it out to the end. So you did, or you tried to. End of story.'

'Yes, of course. It was all about the role and the acting. And with you, too, I'm sure. Wasn't it?' Deep blue eyes pierced her.

She shrugged. 'Of course. What else?'

'Your hamburgers.' The waiter put their plates in front of them, poured the water and left.

She picked up her hamburger and bit into it. 'Oh, this is fabulous!' she exclaimed when she'd swallowed her mouthful. 'I'll really miss American burgers when I go back to England. Nobody makes a burger like an American.'

'Now that sounds serious. Surely the lack of access to the best burgers in the world should make you consider staying in America forever?'

She laughed. 'But life without fish and chips is a dire thought, too.'

He lifted the top half of his bun and liberally applied ketchup to the burger.

'I see that it's my turn again,' he said. 'I'll contribute to our discussion by saying that you can get fish and chips in the States, too. Unfortunately, I suspect that that remark just about exhausts food as a diversionary topic,' he said, replacing the bun. 'What shall we talk about next?'

'As I'm British, how about the weather?'

'Not much scope there—the weather hardly ever changes in this irrigated desert. If that's the only option, I think we'll have to go back to food.'

'All right, then,' she said. 'While we're waiting for the conversational possibilities offered by the apple tart, may I ask you something?'

'Ask away.'

'You've got a photo of a girl with long fair hair next to your computer. Is that your daughter?'

'Yup, that's Carey. She's almost thirteen. She lives with my ex-wife, Cybill. When we first divorced, Carey used to stay with me a lot, and she and Conchita's daughter, Maria, got to be real good friends. But now she's older, she doesn't want to come any more. Or so Cybill says. I expect Cybill's turned her against me—it's the sort of thing she'd do.'

'How unkind of her!' she exclaimed.

'I rather hoped Carey would remember the good times we had together when she was younger, and not let herself be poisoned against me, but I guess she doesn't.'

'I'm really sorry. I shouldn't have said anything.'

'Don't worry about it. It's something I can't change, so I've had to come to terms with the situation.'

'Do they live far away?'

'Nothing's far away, given our freeway system. It takes about an hour and a half for them to get to me.'

'It must always be difficult when a marriage ends and there're children.'

'You're right about that—especially when they split up in a bad way. It's not something I'd ever want to go through again. But enough about me—what about you? Have you ever been married?'

'No. I lived with a family in San Francisco, looking after their two children. It's how I got over from England—the family paid the fare and I worked for them for a year. It showed me what marriage is like first hand, and I saw what an all-day-every-day thing a marriage is. You have to truly love the other person, and I've never felt that way about anyone.'

He smiled. 'Quite the all-rounder, aren't you? Child-minder and secretary *extraordinaire*.'

'Either I misheard, or there was a magic ingredient in that hamburger if you think I'm an *extraordinaire* anything.'

There was a loud burst of noise, and they saw four teenage girls come into the restaurant. The girls caught sight of Matt, stood still and stared.

'I think that's a cue to call for the apple tarts pronto, eat them at speed, and get going.' He signalled for the waiter.

By THE END of the meeting, Leigh felt shattered—her hand ached from non-stop note taking, and she was feeling the effects of her lack of sleep the night before.

The meeting had been with the money men and the production team of his last film, and with everything pointing towards the film being a box-office blockbuster, marketing ideas had flown fast and furiously.

Everyone could see dollar signs in front of their eyes, and with the same production team signed up for the forth-coming Charlie and Ginnie film, that was good news all round.

As they were preparing to leave, a short, balding man went over to speak to Matt, and they stood talking and laughing together for a few minutes. Leigh recognised the man as the producer Bob Lieberman. Then Matt said goodbye to the producer, and he and Leigh returned to the car.

'You did okay this afternoon,' he told her on the journey home. 'For a woman,' he added with a sly grin. 'You kept up, or at least you looked as if you were keeping up, and they liked you. In fact, Bob's asked me to bring you to his party on Saturday. He's always been a sucker for a pretty face. I hadn't intended to go, but I guess I ought to, so we'll go together.'

She felt a sudden panic.

All the women would be stick-thin and glamorous, and she'd stand out like a sore thumb. She'd know only one person there, Matt, and he'd probably be dragged away to talk to someone important as soon as they arrived.

It was one thing for him to get on brilliantly with Fran and her friends, but quite another for her to get on with a movie crowd.

Film people were different from ordinary people. She'd heard it said often enough since she'd come to LA that actors were only as big as their last film, and if you weren't an actor or a top player, no one wanted to waste their time talking to you.

She'd spend the evening standing next to the wall by herself, and that would be so embarrassing.

'It's nice of Bob to ask me to the party. But if it's all right with you, I won't go. I could go to Fran's—I haven't seen her since Joni's party.'

He shook his head. 'It's not all right with me. You're not getting out of this. I went to your party, now it's your turn to go to mine. Apart from the fact that Bob's invited you, it'll be a sight more fun if you're there with me, a spark of sanity in a mad world.'

'Bob's parties must really be something else if they make me look like a spark of sanity!' she exclaimed. She sighed audibly. 'I'll go, then. But don't blame me if I come across as massively boring.'

'Believe me, you won't. It's much more likely that they'll bore you.'

Her hand flew to her mouth. 'I've just thought of a problem. I've nothing to wear for something like that. You'll have to go without me.'

'I'll get you something. Problem solved.'

'Thank you, but no, thank you. Problem remains.'

'Why not let me buy you a dress?' He swung the convertible through the gates that led into Bel Air.

'Because I won't. I'd feel really uncomfortable about it. I wasn't hinting—I was stating a fact.'

'I know that. I didn't for one minute think it was anything else. But you must look upon it as part of your salary. The party is business for me. Bob's asked you to come with me, which makes you being with me business, too.'

'So?'

'So it's obviously my responsibility to see you've got something suitable to wear. Also that you get overtime for working after hours—but we can sort that out later. Tomorrow morning, you must go to a little place I can recommend on Rodeo Drive. They'll fix you up with a dress, which'll be tax deductible. I don't see the problem.'

'When you put it like that, I suppose it sounds sort of fair.'

The car pulled into the drive and stopped. He was still smiling in satisfaction as they got out.

11

───────

As soon as she was back in her office, she phoned Fran and told her about the party.

'I'm dreading it,' she finished.

'But you'll see really big stars!'

'I work for one. The novelty's worn off.'

'You're nuts, honey. It'll be brilliant. What are you wearing?'

'I don't know yet.' She told Fran what Matt had said about the dress. 'Should I let him buy it?'

'Of course, you should. It's a work thing and you have to look good. You can't wear your normal clothes.'

Leigh burst out laughing. 'Well, thank you, friend.'

She heard Fran giggle at the other end of the line. 'You know what I mean.'

'Don't worry, we're still friends. Anyway, what's new with you?'

'Hey, hold on, Leigh! You don't get to change the topic that easily. I want to hear how you're getting on with the dishy Mr Hunter. We all liked him and thought the two of you looked great together.'

'He's fine, I suppose. He's turning out to be a reasonable boss and we seem to get on quite well. But there's no two of us in the way that you mean. He could have any woman he wanted.'

'I hear what you're saying,' Fran soothed. 'But *you* could be that any woman.'

'Get a grip, Fran. This is not a romantic novel, where an actor falls in love with his secretary in the flutter of a false eyelash. This is real life.'

'He's taking you to the party, isn't he?'

'Only because Bob Lieberman asked him to.'

'And you really think that someone as powerful as Matt Hunter would take his secretary to a party just because a producer asked him to? He doesn't obey producers, honey, he *chooses* them. He does what he wants. No, Leigh, you're going to the party because Matt wants you to go with him, and for no other reason.'

'You do talk rubbish, Fran. It's just as well I've got to go now. Matt will be here soon—the thing with the production company is heating up and he might have something for me to do. Speak later.'

As she hung up the phone, a shadow momentarily blocked the sunlight.

She stood up, an expectant smile on her face, but it was Van who pulled open the glass doors and stepped into the office.

'Hello, Van. I thought you were Matt.' She sat down.

'If only,' he said with a smile.

Both laughed.

He sat down on the chair next to Leigh's desk, crossed one slender leg with the other, and brushed an imaginary speck of dust from the knee of his dark grey trousers.

'Actually, in a way I *am* Matt. He asked me to fill you in

about your shopping expedition tomorrow. He says you should take the whole day off, if necessary. Here's what you need to know.' He put a piece of paper on her desk. 'Armando will drive you. It'll save you from having to find a place to leave the car. I thought I'd convey those happy tidings in person.'

'That's very kind of both you and Matt. When I've typed up the notes from today's meeting, I'll be up-to-date with my work so I'll have a clear conscience about tomorrow. I'd hate to go out leaving anything still not done.'

'Your diligence is admirable, Leigh.' He gave her a coy smile. 'But it isn't all work, I believe. I understand that you and Matt are going to Lieberman's party, hence the shopping trip.'

She groaned aloud. 'Yes, we are. To be honest, though, I'm not looking forward to it, but Mr Lieberman invited me.'

'I'm sure you'll enjoy it. He's a powerful man—it's good to keep on the right side of him.'

She pulled a face. 'Now I'm even more scared!'

Van stood up. 'You've nothing to worry about, Leigh. I'm sure you'll triumph.'

BUYING the dress proved to be great fun.

Leigh phoned Fran early in the morning, and asked if she was free to go shopping with her as she could use her advice. Fran jumped at the suggestion, and they arranged to meet outside the shop.

Armando dropped Leigh at the shop a few minutes ahead of Fran, and she stood in excitement, waiting for Fran, enjoying as she did so the light breeze ruffling the fronds at the top of the tall, slender trunks of the palm trees that flanked the wide road.

She knew Rodeo Drive very well. Many a time, she'd walked along it, gazing with yearning at the items on display in the windows of the stylish stores that lined both sides of the street, but never for one moment had she imagined that one day she, herself, would be going into one of those shops and choosing a dress.

When Fran arrived, they went into the store, and were shown to a velvet-covered sofa, and given a glass of crisp white wine. Sipping their wine, they sat feeling very self-conscious as models glided past them in a variety of lovely dresses.

All the assistants were extremely courteous and friendly, and they gradually started to relax, and by the end of the parade had picked out several dresses for Leigh to try.

Leaving Fran in the showroom, Leigh went into the plush fitting room and slipped into the dress that had caught her eye the moment she'd seen it. She turned and stared at her reflection in the mirror, and gasped.

In flame red silk, with pencil thin straps, the dress lightly skimmed her body and fell below her knees to mid-calf. The rich red lustre dramatically set off her auburn hair, and it was hard to believe that the woman staring back at her from the glass was really her.

Feeling suddenly shy, she went out to Fran.

Fran's eyes were eloquent.

'I'll take this one,' Leigh told the assistant. 'I don't need to try on anything else.'

But Matt had included instructions for her to choose shoes and a bag, and when she left, she had three items to sign for. Picking up the carrier bag, she tucked her arm into Fran's and went out into the bright sunlight of Rodeo Drive where Armando was waiting.

'I could get used to this,' Fran remarked cheerfully as

they sat in the back of the car while Armando drove them to the restaurant where Matt had arranged for them to have lunch. '*I'm* glad you're going to the party, even if you're not.'

THE REST of the week flew by and Leigh didn't have time to think about the party. With the purchase of the company imminent, Matt had a number of meetings with the board of Heartlands, after which she had what felt like an endless stream of notes to type up. Finally, though, Saturday evening arrived.

As she fastened her dress, a sense of excitement stirred within her. It didn't really matter if she didn't speak to anyone—she was going to a Hollywood party, in what she was sure would be an amazing house, and where she'd see lots of famous faces, and the food was bound to be good.

It was going to be an unforgettable evening, and one she was unlikely ever to repeat.

She slid into her high red heels, hoping that she'd be able to keep her balance as they were higher than she'd worn for a long time, applied a touch of lip-gloss and stared at her reflection in the mirror.

The red dress was absolutely perfect, and she felt a million dollars.

Fran had been right when she'd told her over lunch that the dress had the Wow! factor. She knew that she'd never before in her life looked as she looked that night, and she couldn't wait to see Matt and hear what he had to say when he saw her.

He hadn't yet seen the dress.

When she'd returned from the shopping trip, he'd asked if she'd found what she wanted, and she'd told him that she had, but that was all she'd said—he didn't even know the colour.

She glanced at her watch. It was time she got going—Matt might already be waiting in the entrance hall. She took a few deep breaths to steady her nerves at the thought of the car journey there and back, throughout which she'd be sitting spine-tinglingly close to her boss, and then she went over to her bed and picked up her new evening bag.

On her way to the entrance hall, she passed Matt's study.

His door was slightly ajar, she noticed, and she heard a movement inside the room. She knew that Van was out, so it must be Matt, she thought in surprise. He must have popped in there for something before meeting her in the hall. Well, there was no time like the present—she'd show him her dress.

Pushing the door further open, she stepped into the room, closed her eyes, stretched her arms out wide, and a smile on her face, twirled around on the spot, her bag dangling from her fingers.

'Well, how do I look?' she cried in glee.

'Gross!'

She abruptly stopped twirling. Her eyes flew open and her arms fell to her sides.

Standing in front of Matt's desk, staring at her with undisguised hostility, was a young girl of about twelve or thirteen, with long fair hair that was tied in bunches.

On her face was the identical frown that Leigh had seen on Matt Hunter's face the night he'd walked into the cabana and found her with Van.

'Absolutely gross,' the girl repeated.

12

Leigh took a step forward. 'Hello, Carey.'

Carey pressed back against the desk. She stared at Leigh with undisguised suspicion. 'Who are you? How d'you know my name?'

'I'm Leigh Carter, your father's secretary. I'm working for him while Tom's away. Your father's got a photo of you on his desk so that's how I know who you are. Look behind you and you'll see it.'

'Why d'you talk like that? Is it put on? If it is, I'd drop it —it sounds gross.'

'I come from London, in England. Have you ever been there?'

'Only once, I'm glad to say. When I was real little. It rained all the time. The weather in England's real skanky.'

'I'm sorry.'

Leigh frowned. How come she was apologising to Carey for the English weather! Carey should be apologising to her for her rudeness!

'Why're you all dressed up like that? Where are you going?'

'I'm sorry, Carey, but that isn't really any of your business.'

Carey glared at her. 'Servants shouldn't speak to their employers like that,' she said haughtily. 'You work for my dad, so in a way you work for me. You're rude. I could get my dad to fire you.'

Leigh sensed a movement behind her, and turned as Matt came into the study.

'Oh, there you are, Carey.' There was relief in his voice. 'I didn't know where you'd got to. Who am I meant to be firing?'

'I'm afraid she means me, Matt. Carey and I seem to have got off on the wrong foot.'

His smile embraced them both. 'Then let's get you both on to the right feet, shall we?'

She smiled back. A sudden thought struck her, and her smile faded. 'How did Carey get here? Is Mrs Harding here, too?'

'Nope. She dropped Carey and her bags on the drive, and left at once. It seems that Carey's staying a while. The whole thing's a total surprise to me.' He smiled quickly at his daughter. 'But a very pleasant surprise.' He turned back to Leigh. 'It's typical of Cybill. She can be thoroughly thoughtless.'

'D'you mind! That's my mother you're talking about!'

'Yup, you're right, Carey. I shouldn't have said that. I guess I was put out because it was unexpected, but I'm real glad you're here. The timing's bad, though. We're just about to go out.'

'You going out with *her*?' Carey nodded towards Leigh, an expression of surprised disgust on her face.

'My secretary's name is Leigh. Kindly remember your

manners, young lady. There's no need to be rude. Leigh and I have been invited to a party at Bob Lieberman's.'

'Bob slimy Lieberman! Yuk! He came to our house once. He's so gross.'

'Gross or not, you're going to have to come along, too.'

'Me go and meet a lot of boring old people, who are all talking about boring old things? No way. Get real, Dad. You go and be bored if you want, and you can take *Leigh* with you, but I'm gonna see Conchita and Maria. It'll be neat to hang out with Maria again—I bet she'll be real surprised to see me.'

'You won't find them, I'm afraid. They're out for the evening. And so's Van. That's why you must come with us.'

'Then I'll stay in on my own. I'm old enough. I'm almost thirteen—but like you'd remember. Cybill lets me stay on my own.'

'What's this with Cybill! What's wrong with Mom?'

'She doesn't like it. She says it makes her feel old.'

'Well, you're not staying behind on your own and that's that.'

Father and daughter glared at each other.

'We don't have to go to the party,' Leigh ventured.

Matt and Carey turned to her simultaneously. Four intense blue eyes stared at her.

Carey turned back to her father. She scowled accusingly. 'You don't trust me, Matt. That's what it is.'

'It's Pop, or Dad, or Sir. But whatever it is, it isn't Matt. As for a title making a person feel old, at this precise minute I don't need any kind of title to make me feel old.'

'We don't have to go to the party,' Leigh repeated. 'I'm sure Mr Lieberman would understand if I called and explained the situation.'

Matt ran his fingers through his hair. 'I guess you'll have

to do that, then. Shame. I'd kinda got used to the idea of the party. Well then, when you've rung Bob, you might as well ring Lawry's and book a table for three. Make it an hour from now. We've gotta eat, and Conchita's out. I'm sorry about the party, Leigh.'

'There's no need to apologise. The party really doesn't matter.'

He glanced at Carey. 'You can be putting your things away, Carey. Armando's out so I'll take your bags to your room.' He started to go towards the door.

'I don't wanna go out.'

Matt stopped in his tracks. 'What's the devil's the matter now? Is it that you've already eaten? Or that you don't eat? Or that you only eat brown rice and alfalfa? You've already played havoc with the evening, so what could possibly be the problem now?'

'I've not eaten, *Pop*, but I don't wanna go out. People always stare at us, and they always watch you when you eat. It makes me feel like a dork.'

Her jaw set in a stubborn line.

He gestured helplessly. 'Conchita's out and we've gotta eat. I'm sorry, but we're going out, and that's that.' He continued towards the door.

Leigh turned towards Carey to ask if there was anything she needed. The expression on Carey's face stopped her short.

Carey was gazing at her father's retreating back with eyes full of wistful yearning.

The stroppiness had fallen away and she looked like the twelve-year-old that she was.

In a flash, Leigh realised that Carey's brashness was nothing more than a front. She was nervous about being with her father again, and she didn't want to share him with the public at large.

Her heart reached out to the young girl.

'I could cook a meal, Matt. I'm not a brilliant cook, but I looked after two kids for a year. If you want, I can make you and Carey an omelette or something.'

His eyes filled with relief. 'Well, if you really think you could rustle up something for the three of us, and you don't mind?'

'It's not rocket science. It'll be fun. I'd better get changed first, though. You can help me in the kitchen, if you want, Carey. Can you cook?'

The wistful yearning vanished fast. Carey stuck her nose in the air.

'Nope. I've never learnt and I don't want to. That's why people have servants. You work for my dad, so you do it. I'll be in my room till the food's ready.' She took a step towards the door.

'Stay where you are, young lady,' Matt said firmly. 'You'll apologise for your rudeness just now. It was completely uncalled for.'

'I'm sorry,' Carey muttered sullenly.

'And now you'll get changed and get into the kitchen or you won't be eating at all tonight. You're lucky that Leigh is willing to cook for us. It's not what she's employed to do— she's doing it out of kindness.'

'Don't be too sure of that, Matt,' she said lightly. 'You haven't tasted my cooking yet.'

Carey opened her mouth, caught her father's eye and closed it. Brushing past her father, she stalked out of the study.

'Wear something old in case you get dirty,' Leigh called after her.

'This is real nice of you, Leigh. I'm very grateful. We'll eat in the den tonight—I think Carey would prefer that. I'll get her bags, and then while you're doing the meal, I'll ring Bob.' He hesitated. 'I'm sorry about Carey's rudeness. She never used to be like that.'

'Don't think twice about it. She's a girl who's not seen enough of her father in recent years. She wants to be with you and no one else. I'm someone else. She'll be fine in a bit. You'll see.'

'I sure hope you're right.' He hesitated. 'But before you go, I've just gotta tell you how truly lovely you look,' he said quietly. 'You're absolutely beautiful, Leigh.'

And he went out of his study.

HALF AN HOUR LATER, Leigh had exchanged the flame red dress for her favourite jeans and a white T-shirt, and had wrapped herself in one of Conchita's aprons. When Carey joined her, she insisted that Carey do the same. Acting as if she'd never touched an apron before, Carey reluctantly tied it around her waist.

'You'd never catch my mom in the kitchen,' she said, sniffing.

'That so?' Leigh remarked. 'Then I'm sorry for your mother—cooking's fun. Anyway, I had a look in the cupboards while I was waiting for you, and there's not much that Conchita doesn't have, but we must try not to take anything that looks as if it's earmarked for a particular meal.'

'Whatever.'

'We'll take some eggs,' Leigh went on, opening the pantry door, 'a few onions, some potatoes, green peppers and tomatoes. That should make a nice omelette, don't you think?'

Carey gave a loud sigh.

'Right.' Leigh put everything on the long wooden table in the centre of the kitchen. 'It'll be a sort of Spanish omelette, followed by some Baskin-Robbins ice cream. Conchita always has a tub of English Toffee in the freezer—it's my favourite. How does that sound to you?'

'Like I care,' was the reply.

Her impatience growing, Leigh forced herself to bite back a sharp riposte and tried to remember instead the yearning on Carey's face.

'Get peeling, then,' she said, and she handed Carey several potatoes and a peeler.

'No way!' Carey stepped back from the table. 'What d'you think I am? Mom would be real angry if I told her I'd had to do a servant's work. She'd never let me come again.'

Leigh stopped slicing the peppers and stared at Carey. 'You trying to blackmail me, Carey? If I make you help with the meal, you'll get your own back by making sure you're never allowed to visit your dad again? Is that it? D'you think your dad would be the only one to lose out if that happened?'

'You sound weird. I don't know what you're talking about,' Carey muttered sullenly.

'Yes, you do. Now, if you want to eat tonight, you're going to have to help. Alternatively, you can go to bed right now. Or you can go your room and do your homework. Or don't they give you any in charm school?'

Inwardly, she kicked herself. She shouldn't have sunk to Carey's level—the girl was only twelve, after all.

Finding a strange woman in her father's house must have been a shock—she probably hadn't even known that

Tom was away. She was older than Carey and should have been more understanding, and more in control of her tongue. She must be more careful in the future.

'Simple choice, Carey,' Leigh said, softening her voice. 'What's it going to be?'

A sulky expression on her face, Carey picked up a potato and ran the peeler across it.

'What's your school like?' Leigh asked after they'd been working in silence for a few minutes.

'It's gross.'

'What's your favourite lesson?'

'Study periods.'

'Is the school far from where you live?'

'What's this—a cross-examination?'

'No, it's called a conversation. It's what grown-ups do. It's infinitely better than an exchange of rudeness. Listening to rudeness is boring, and I don't do bored, so grow up, will you?'

'What planet did my dad get you from?'

Leigh smiled at her with exaggerated sweetness. 'I could most definitely say the same to you.' And she took the peeled potatoes from Carey and cut them into slices.

Carey stood watching, a scowl on her face.

'Why don't you whisk the eggs, Carey?'

'Whatever.'

'I'll do the onions,' Leigh said. 'I hate peeling onions as they always make me cry. As soon as you've done the eggs and I've done the onions, we'll heat some oil in the pan.'

'Those kids you looked after,' Carey said. 'I bet they thought you were a dork.'

'I doubt it. They were lovely, well-mannered children, who were a pleasure to be with. I really enjoyed my year with them.'

'They sound boring to me.'

'Being polite isn't boring. Make a tape of yourself one day and listen to how you sound when you speak to someone like me. Then you'll know what boring is. Gross is the word that will likely spring to your mind when you hear yourself. Now let's get this omelette done, shall we?'

'I'M afraid it all looks a bit homespun,' Leigh said, coming into the den and putting a large tray on the low coffee table. Carey followed holding three plates and some cutlery, a bored expression on her face. Leigh took the omelette and basket of bread from the tray and put them on the table.

She straightened up. 'Carey peeled the potatoes, Matt,' she said, smiling at Carey. 'She was a great help.'

Carey gave a dramatic sigh.

'So you're sharing the blame, are you?' Matt said. He peered at the omelette and assumed a face of great nervousness.

Carey glanced at her father, and an involuntary burst of laughter escaped her. 'You should see what you look like, Dad!' she exclaimed. 'It's not *that* bad!'

Quickly rearranging her features into sulky indifference, Carey sat down heavily on the sofa next to her father.

Leigh sat down on the sofa opposite, and shared out the omelette. 'It's certainly colourful. That's because it's got just about everything in it. Hopefully, it'll taste all right. But I've a feeling you won't be sacking Conchita and installing me in her place.'

She took some bread, and offered the basket to Matt and then to Carey. Carey pushed it away from her. She stared at Leigh's plate and wrinkled her nose. 'You're not gonna eat that bread, are you?'

'Why not? I'm hungry, and I love sourdough.'

Carey sniffed. 'Cybill would never eat that. She wouldn't eat the omelette either—there's fat in the yolks. Cook's only allowed to make an omelette with the white part of the egg. She's real slim, my mom is.'

'Your mother doesn't know what she's missing,' Leigh said, spreading a deliberately over-generous portion of butter on her bread.

'She does, but she says nothing tastes as good as being thin.'

'Then she's not tried English Toffee ice cream,' Leigh retorted.

'Speaking as a man, there's a happy medium when it comes to food, Carey,' Matt said, picking up his fork. 'I'm sure most men prefer women who eat. I certainly do. There's nothing pleasant about watching a woman play around with the food on her plate. So eat up, will you, and then you can tell me what you've been up to since we last met. We've a lot of catching up to do.'

'YOU DON'T HAVE to go yet, do you?' Matt asked, leaning back and relaxing as the sound of Carey clattering her way along the corridor to her room died away. 'I don't know about you, but I certainly need to unwind. She's gotten hard work, my Carey.'

Leigh sat back down on the sofa opposite Matt.

'Cybill's obviously trying to make Carey into a clone of herself,' he continued. 'I'm sorry she was so rude to you this evening. I do apologise for that. If it hadn't been her first time here for so long, I'd have stepped on her real hard.'

'Well, I'm glad you didn't. She must be feeling very

strange, being here again, and she needs time to settle. Give her a few days, and I'm certain she'll go back to her old self.'

'I sure hope you're right,' he said fervently. 'It's been a very different evening from the evening I thought it'd be. Bob was fine about everything, by the way,' he said, and he got up and went over to a switch on the wall.

He flicked the switch and the slatted blinds closed. Then he flicked another switch, and subtle lighting filled the den with a warm intimacy.

'It's late. I ought to go now,' Leigh said, standing up as Matt returned to the sofa.

'Don't worry—I won't pounce,' he said wryly. 'Charlie and Ginnie are battened down for the night.'

She sat down again, butterflies fluttering furiously in her stomach.

Annoyed with herself for suddenly feeling so acutely aware of Matt's nearness, she shifted her position, looking everywhere but at the powerful legs stretched lazily out in front of the sofa opposite.

'More wine?' he asked, and he leaned forward and picked up the bottle.

'I'll pass, thanks,' she said. She edged forward on her seat. 'You know, I think I really ought to turn in. I've got a tyrant for a boss and I need to be ready for work at the crack of dawn.'

'Tyrant! You do amaze me!' Matt's eyes opened wide in mock astonishment. 'Whenever I've heard people talk about the man, it's been with words such as "masterful" and "just".'

'You must have misheard them, then,' she said sweetly. '"Merciless" and "cussed" more like.'

They smiled at each other.

'If we'd gone to the party, we'd still be at Bob's,' he said slyly, 'so you're not up any later than you would've been. Surely, you can stay a while longer.' Hopeful blue eyes smiled at her across the coffee table.

She gave in and sank back against the sofa.

'So now you've met my strong-willed Carey,' he said with studied casualness, 'I hope it's not put you off being here.'

Behind his words, she heard an unmistakable anxiety.

'Not in the least,' she said with a reassuring smile. 'There's nothing wrong with being strong-willed. She's almost a teenager and it goes with the territory. I suspect that under the stroppy façade there's a really nice girl.' The longing on Carey's face as she stared after her father sprang into Leigh's mind. 'She definitely wants to be here, Matt. She adores you. I saw her face when she was watching you earlier.'

'I hope you're right. She was such fun when she was a little kid. It's hard to believe she can have changed that much.'

'How long is she staying?'

'Your guess is as good as mine. For ever, if I had my way, but you can't tell with Cybill. That woman's a law unto herself. Frustration about her career will be at the bottom of it. It's much harder for women to get parts in movies as they get older than it is for men, and her career has kind of stalled. She gets work in Italy, but Italy's not Hollywood, and Hollywood is where she wants to be. I imagine that's gotten to her.'

'Why d'you think she's let Carey visit you now?'

'There's bound to be a reason, but don't ask me what it is.' He hesitated. 'But I ought to apologise for myself, Leigh, and not just for Carey. I've been so wound up about Carey that I've not yet thanked you for your help tonight. I'm more grateful than I can say.'

'I hardly did anything.'

'That's not so. You were a big help with Carey, cooking and all that.'

'It wasn't much.'

'It was to me. I don't think I'd have managed without you. In fact, I'm hoping you'll carry on giving me a hand with her for as long as she's here.'

'How d'you mean?' she asked in surprise.

'Well, my deal's close to completion, and the next couple of weeks or so are going to be pretty wild. It means I won't have as much time for Carey as I'd like. I'm worried she might be bored and not want to come again, and I'm wondering if you'd be a sort of friend to her—take her out occasionally, or keep an eye on her if she's swimming. You know the kind of thing.'

'If you think that's the best way I can be of help.'

'I do. Whatever she might think, she's too young to be left on her own all day. And you could teach her some manners while you were at it. And maybe an English accent —it's kinda neat. At least it is when you're not having a go at me,' he added with a smile. 'Well, what d'you say?'

'Shouldn't I be working on the takeover?'

'In an ideal world, yes. Especially as I have to admit, you've got those superior skills you bragged about.' Leigh threw a cushion at him and he ducked, laughing.

'But it's not an ideal world,' he continued, 'not with the takeover and Carey rubbing shoulders with each other. You can't do everything, and if you're tied up with Carey, you won't be able to be in the office. Van can arrange for extra secretarial help. And as for the takeover, Van picked up the key threads before Tom went off to Chicago, and he'll just have to take on a bit more of the practical side than he'd expected. But he's a friend, and he'll want to help. So, d'you think you could help me with her?'

'Of course, I can. Or as Carey would say, whatever.'

He let out a sigh of relief. 'Thanks, Leigh. That's a massive load off my mind.'

She stood up. 'Well, if I'm going to be up to sparring with Carey tomorrow, I'm going to need all my strength, and I'm definitely getting off to bed now.'

'Fair enough,' he said, and he stood up. 'I'll see you in the morning, then. I'm meeting some business folk for brunch, but I'll try and catch Carey before I leave, assuming she's up in time, that is.'

'I'm sure she'd like that. Good night, Matt.'

'Good night, Leigh, and thanks again for everything.'

'You're welcome,' she said, and she went across to the door and opened it.

'Leigh,' she heard him call, and she turned back to him.

'I just wanted to tell you again how lovely you looked in your red dress. Really lovely.'

Her eyes met his. For a long moment both stood motionless, their eyes locked.

'Okay,' she said. 'Night.'

And she stepped into the corridor, and shut the door behind her.

13

Matt and Carey were already on the terrace when Leigh emerged from the house the following morning.

When she saw that Matt was talking to Carey, she hesitated, thinking it might be better for her to eat indoors rather than intrude on their first morning together. But before she could turn to go, Matt saw her.

She was pretty sure that she saw a look of relief on his face.

'Come and join us,' he called.

Yes, he definitely looked somewhat harassed, she thought in amusement. So she wasn't the only one receiving the Carey treatment. She sat down opposite him, and he poured her a glass of chilled orange juice.

'I've just been explaining the situation to Carey, telling her how the two of you will spend some time together when I can't be around. That's okay, isn't it, Carey?'

Carey turned a sullen face to Leigh, and grunted.

'Aha, here's Conchita. What perfect timing,' Matt said as Conchita appeared with a large tray.

Conchita's face was wreathed in smiles as she came across to the table, put the tray on a stand and gave them each a plate covered with thin rashers of Danish bacon and an egg cooked sunny side up. Then she put a dish of blueberry pancakes smothered in melting butter and maple syrup in the centre of the table, and a pot of coffee next to it.

'We have to build you up, Miss Carey. You too thin and pale. You need flesh and colour. You see Maria later, when she get back from my sister. She got plenty flesh and colour.'

Smiling contentedly, she went back to the kitchen.

Leigh and Matt picked up their knife and fork. Carey sat still, her eyes moving between her plate and the dish of pancakes.

'You'll upset Conchita if you don't eat your breakfast,' Matt said as he started eating. 'Is that what you want?'

Carey picked up her knife and fork and cut a small piece of bacon.

'If Mom could see me now, she'd just die. You are what you eat, Carey,' she mimicked in a high-pitched voice. 'A moment on the lips, forever on the hips, Carey,' she continued.

Both Matt and Leigh burst out laughing. An expression of pleased surprise swept across Carey's face. She swiftly wiped it off.

'You don't have to worry, Carey,' Leigh told her. 'You're naturally slim. And even if you weren't, you'd soon work off the calories at your age. A few lengths of the pool would instantly burn them up.'

Carey sniffed. 'I don't do swimming.'

'Since when?' Matt exclaimed in surprise. 'You and Maria used to be in the pool all day—we couldn't get you out. Maria's an excellent swimmer, and you weren't that bad.'

'That was then; this is now.'

Matt and Leigh exchanged looks across the table.

He glanced at his watch and started to fold up his napkin. 'I'd like to explore this further, Carey, but I'm afraid I have to leave now. Perhaps you can get to the bottom of Carey's sudden aversion to swimming, Leigh.'

'I've changed my mind, Dad—I don't want her here. You can take her with you.'

He stood up and looked down at Carey. 'You know I'd like to stay with you, but I can't. And you know you can't stay on your own. So who are you getting at now, Carey—me or Leigh?'

'Whoever,' she muttered sullenly.

'Well, at least you're not choosy! That's something, I suppose.' He leaned over and kissed Carey on the forehead.

Leigh saw the fleeting delight on Carey's face.

'Bye, honey.' He tapped Carey lightly on the nose. 'It's great to have you here, trouble though you are. Have a good day and go easy on Leigh, won't you?' He turned to Leigh. 'I'll be home the minute I can.'

And he was gone.

Carey emptied her plate, pushed it away from her and sighed loudly. 'Haven't you got something to do, like a mushroom to stuff or a broomstick to mend?'

'Like it or not, you're what I'm going to do today, Carey. So it's up to you—we can have a fun time together or we can be rude to each other all day and not have any fun. You choose. The ball's in your court.'

'I'll have my fun time with Maria, thank you very much. You can do whatever you want.'

'You're boring me again, Carey,' Leigh said with dramatic weariness. 'I know you'd rather be with your dad, and I know he'd rather be with you—but he's got work like you wouldn't believe at the moment. How's he going to feel if you make things harder for him by not doing as he asks? Are you deliberately trying to upset him?'

Carey didn't answer.

'Well?' Leigh repeated.

'No, of course I'm not. I'm here, aren't I?'

'But are you here for the right reason?'

'You're loopy, you are.'

'All I ask is that you think about the effects of your behaviour on your dad. But let's move on, shall we? What would you like to do today?'

'Chill out with Maria.'

'Okay. It's getting quite hot so why don't we have a swim while we wait for Maria to join us? Your father said you were quite good. We could have a race. It might be fun.'

'You're obsessed with fun, you are! And I told you I don't do swimming. Cybill says the sun makes you look old. If you go in the pool, the sun gets you through the water.'

'We can use the indoor pool, then. On a hot day, it's better than nothing. Or are you at risk of aging there as well, as the sun comes in through the glass roof?'

She watched Carey's eyes move longingly towards the pool. The blue water was glittering in the morning sun. She felt a wave of sympathy for Carey. 'What happens when your friends come over to play? Do they go swimming while you stay indoors?'

'They don't come to *play*,' Carey said scornfully. 'We're not babies. We hang out together.'

'So what happens when you're all hanging out near a pool, and it's hot?'

'I'm not allowed in the water. The other kids muck around in the pool, drink cream sodas and everything, but I have to sit there, all covered up under a big hat and an even bigger umbrella, with a glass of water in my hand. Not even fizzy water 'cos that's bad for you, too,' she added in sudden indignation.

'So obviously, no cola.'

'Definitely no cola—I'm never ever allowed to drink it. The other kids do, though, and they look fine to me.'

Leigh stifled the desire to laugh at the picture Carey painted of herself. 'Your mother only wants what she thinks is best for you. But if you *do* want to go in the outdoor pool for once, we can smother you in sunscreen.'

A shadow blocked the light from their table.

Both looked up at the same moment.

Van Attwood was standing beside them, his mouth smiling down at Carey.

'Hello, Carey,' he said, pulling out a chair and sitting down between them. 'It's real good to see you again, honey. When Matt phoned and told me you were here, I came at once to say hello.' The smile widened.

'It's not that long since you last said hello,' Carey snapped irritably. 'You're always at our house or talking to Mom on the phone.'

'I don't know about always,' he said, and he gave a short, mirthless laugh. 'Occasionally I speak to your mother; that's all. But it's invariably a pleasure when I do.'

'I sure dunno why—she's forever in a strop,' she said sulkily.

Leigh felt a sudden alarm.

Instinct told her it would be better if Carey didn't antagonise Van, as Matt was going to need Van's help throughout Carey's stay. She glanced at him nervously, but he was smiling indulgently at Carey. If he was annoyed, he was certainly hiding it well, she thought.

'If your mother seems a little on edge at times,' he said

smoothly, 'it's probably that the negotiations about her contract are preoccupying her. I understand that she's talking about a three-film contract with an Italian studio, which would be a tremendous coup for her. She's bound to be worried that something will go wrong.'

'Huh? What're you talking about? What contract? I'm not gonna go to Italy; no way!'

'It's early days. She's probably waiting till there's something definite to tell you. We'll all have to be patient. And while we are, is there anything I can do to make your stay more pleasant, honey?'

Carey opened her mouth to answer. Leigh had a sudden premonition of what she was about to say, and got in there first.

'That's very kind of you, Van, but we're fine. If we need anything, though, we won't hesitate to ask. We're about to go for a swim.'

'For a swim?' He raised a thin eyebrow in Carey's direction. 'I'm not sure what your mother would say.' He looked back at Leigh. 'But of course, it's up to you what you allow her to do, Leigh. I don't really see Cybill often enough to know the rules she likes to enforce.' He stood up, smoothed down his trousers and gave them both a slight bow. 'You two girls enjoy the day. I won't detain you any longer.'

'Yuk, what a slimeball!' Carey said, wrinkling her nose in distaste as she watched him disappear through the glass doors. 'He says he doesn't come often, but he does. He's always at our house.'

Leigh stared at her in surprise.

'I dunno why Mom puts up with him,' Carey continued, 'but she seems to like him. He's gross, if you ask me. Maybe it's 'cos he's always talking like she and Dad are gonna get back together. As if.' She rolled her eyes towards the sky.

'Tom said Van's been a good friend of your father for many years, and he's been extremely helpful to me. Slimeball's a bit hard, don't you think?'

'You should hear him when he's with Mom! He's always sucking up to her, and that's slimy.'

Leigh knew she ought not to pursue this further, but should steer the conversation away from Cybill and Matt towards something considerably less personal.

'And what does your mother say when Van hints about her getting back with your father?' she asked.

Knowing what you should do, and doing it, were two different things, she thought ruefully

'She'd sure like it, but not 'cos she wants to be with Dad —they used to fight all the time—but 'cos she wants to be Hollywood A-list again.'

'I'm sure you're wrong about Van thinking they might get back together,' Leigh remarked, ignoring her conscience and pursuing the subject further.

'I'm not. I heard them talking when Van's been at our house, didn't I? But it's not gonna happen. Mom and Pop will never get back together.'

An anxiety that Leigh hadn't known had been building up in her, drained away.

'Right, Carey. Just say what you'd like to do today—it's *your* day. If you don't want to swim, we can do something else while we wait for Maria to get back.'

'I've had a breakfast that would make Mom go mental, so why stop there? The pool looks good. But I'm not going in if I have to wear a hat. I'd feel like a dork,' she added belligerently.

'Believe me, I wasn't about to suggest it. A swim it is, then. Did you bring a swimsuit with you?'

'Just one. It's gross, but it's better than nothing.'

'I'll bring out the sunscreen. You need to put plenty on. Wear your swimsuit today, and perhaps we'll pick up another when we're in Beverly Hills.'

'Is that what we're doing tomorrow?'

'I thought we might go there, but only if you want.'

'Won't you have some pencils to sharpen or something?'

'Your father said you were the priority, and he's going to get someone in to do my work if necessary. He might even go mad and buy in a box of pre-sharpened pencils. Who knows!'

'You're loopy, you are.' She leaned back against her chair and sighed. 'But I suppose we could have a swim. We've gotta do something. Maria can swim, too, can't she, when she gets back?'

'If that's okay with Conchita. But to go back to the next few days, perhaps you and I can have a girlie day out on one of the days and get our hair done. And we could go to a nail bar. There's a great one on Rodeo,' Leigh added, warming to her theme.

'That'd be cool, I suppose!' Carey coiled her long fair hair on top of her head, and assumed a sophisticated face. 'Can I get a dress, too? Everything Mom buys me makes me look like a baby.'

'That's up to your father. And also, I've got some good friends you can meet, if you want. Your father came with me to my friend Fran's party. I'm sure he wouldn't mind if I took you to meet them. Fran's got lots of interesting things in her house.'

'Do your friends talk all weird like you?'

'Not at all—they're American.' She paused, and enjoyed the thought of meeting up with Fran. For a few hours, she might lighten the burden of keeping Carey amused. 'D'you think you'd like to meet them at some point?' she asked hopefully.

'Whatever,' Carey mumbled. Then she glanced slyly at Leigh. 'So you went out with my dad, did you? To that Fran's. D'you think Dad's good looking? The girls at my school think he is.'

'I didn't go out with him in the way that you mean. He invited himself along when I was off to meet my friends. He's my boss. I don't think of him in any other way.'

'Huh! Like I believe you.'

'What you believe is neither here nor there. So, are we going to swim today?'

Carey eyed the pool. 'I guess so. I'll go and get changed and go in the water now,' she said, and she got up.

'Bring a book when you come back. It's less than an hour since breakfast. We must wait a full hour before going into the pool.'

'God, you sound like my mom!' Carey exclaimed.

'Don't swear, Carey. And I've no desire to sound like anyone's mum. But I don't mind sounding like a friend.'

'Nope, you nag. Friends don't nag. You're like a mom,' Carey insisted, and she disappeared into the house.

Van's arrival had been a real stroke of luck, Leigh thought. The focus of Carey's hostility had moved from her to Van.

For the moment, at least.

14

———

Carey was already sitting at a parasol-shaded table when Leigh reached the pool. She sat down next to Carey and passed her the sunscreen.

'In fifteen minutes, we can go in the water,' she said, opening her book, and Carey did the same.

The moment the time was up, Carey jumped into the shallow end of the pool and started swimming across the width.

Leigh stood on the paved surround, watching Carey swim from side to side with the awkwardness of someone who hadn't been swimming for quite a while. Then she threw off her robe, went up to the deep end, dived in and swam over to Carey. Swimming alongside her, she kept pace with her.

'You swim well,' Carey gasped, swallowing a mouthful of water.

'So will you before long.' She turned on to her back and treaded water. 'You'll soon be able to swim like a Californian again, and who better to help you back to that standard than a Brit. It's like riding a bicycle—you never really forget how to do it. You'll be up to speed in no time, literally.'

Before long, Carey had lengthened her reach and was breathing at the correct rhythm for her stroke, and they were swimming comfortably across the pool, side by side.

'I'm ready for that race now,' Carey said.

'Carey!' they heard a girl shriek from the other side of the garden.

They stopped swimming and stared in the direction of the voice. A dark-haired girl of Carey's age was bounding over the grass towards the pool, her hair flying wildly.

'Maria!' Carey screamed with delight, and swum as fast as she could to the side of the pool, all attempt at style abandoned.

She pulled herself out of the water, ran to Maria and they flung their arms around each other, jumping up and down and laughing hysterically. Then they drew back, each looking curiously at the other's face, and then they hugged again.

'D'you want to come and see my room?' Maria asked excitedly.

'You bet!' Carey tucked her arm in Maria's and started to walk away. Suddenly she stopped and looked back. 'I can, can't I?'

'Of course. Have fun,' Leigh called up to her.

Carey rolled her eyes. 'You and your fun!'

'Carey can have lunch with me, can't she? Please.' Maria's large brown eyes pleaded with Leigh.

'All right. But don't get in Conchita's way, Carey. You'll find me in the house when you've finished with Maria and Conchita.'

'You should've come here more often, Carey,' she heard

Maria say accusingly just before their voices were lost in the distance.

She swam slowly to the steps and got out of the pool.

Bending over to pick up her robe, she had the strangest feeling of being watched. Her skin prickling, she straightened up. Shading her eyes against the rays of the sun, she stared around the garden.

But the terrace and veranda were empty, and there didn't appear to be anyone among the trees at the back of the cabana, nor anywhere else in the garden as far as she could see.

She must have been mistaken, she decided, and she slipped into her robe, tied the belt tightly, picked up her book and Carey's, and started to walk slowly back to the house.

How strange that Van should be as friendly with Cybill Harding as he was, she mused as she strolled along, and how peculiar that he didn't want anyone to know.

Clearly, Matt and his ex-wife were hardly the best of friends, and with Van being as close to Matt as he was, she thought he would've cut all ties with Cybill long ago.

That he hadn't suggested that he might be interested in her himself, unlikely though that sounded. And it was even more unlikely to be for that reason if Carey was right about Van encouraging Cybill to think that she and Matt might get back together.

Carey must surely be mistaken. Van must know better than anyone else that Matt had no time at all for Cybill.

She shook her head. Something was wrong somewhere, but as it was none of her business what Matt and Cybill did or didn't do, she was going to put it out of her mind.

15

———

As Matt had thought would happen, he was tied up with numerous meetings throughout the following couple of weeks—if it wasn't pre-production work on the new film, it was matters to do with Heartlands—and he was hardly at home at all during the day.

With Leigh keeping an eye on Carey in Matt's absence, Van was having to get in extra office help on an almost daily basis.

The easiest thing in the circumstances, Leigh had decided after the first day with another temp in the house, was to make sure that she and Carey were out of the way for as much of the day as was possible.

Fortunately for Leigh, it turned out that Carey had seen next to nothing of Los Angeles in the past, so she'd jumped at the easiest option for filling Carey's day, and they'd gone almost daily into the city to explore it, often with Maria, too.

. . .

'THERE CAN'T BE MUCH LEFT to see,' Matt said one morning when he and Leigh were having a quick breakfast, and she'd just told him that they were off to the city again that day.

'You've covered just about every nook and cranny of LA,' he said. 'Carey's having a swell time, thanks to you, and she's almost back to her old self.'

'I'm enjoying it, too. But I do feel guilty at being out of the office so much. After all, I'm here to help you, as I seem to recall you once reminded me.'

Matt grinned at her. 'That feels a very long time ago. And anyway, when you do something for Carey, you *are* helping me.' He poured himself another coffee. 'So where are you heading today?'

Their first girlie day in Beverly Hills had been such a great success that both she and Carey were strongly in favour of another such day, Leigh told him. So that day, they were going to go to Kim-Ly's nail bar on Rodeo.

They'd intended to go there the first time they were in Beverly Hills, but they'd spent so much time looking for clothes for Carey that day that they hadn't been able to fit in a manicure, and Carey was keen that they didn't forget about it.

And then the next day, she told him, they were going to go to the Farmers' Market, and on to Nate'n Al's for lunch. Carey had told her that Nate'n Al was one of the places she used to go to with Matt when she was little, and she very much wanted to go there again.

'Sounds real good to me,' he said wistfully. 'I sure wish I could join you, but I can't.'

'I hope you think that this evening sounds good, too,' Leigh said lightly. 'You've got the starring role. You're barbe-cuing. It was Carey's idea.'

'Ouch! She's had better ideas. I've yet to make a really good burger.'

'I don't believe you.'

'It's true, I'm afraid. Like lots of things, it's not something you do on your own, so I'm totally out of practice.'

'Well, you're not on your own tonight. It'll be you, me and Carey, and Van if he's around.'

'That reminds me of something I meant to tell you.' He glanced at her above the rim of his coffee cup. 'When I was talking to Carey last night, she asked me what I thought of you,' he said, his tone conversational.

Leigh picked up her cup and clutched it tightly.

'It's how kids talk.' She attempted a laugh. 'And Carey's not one to hold back. She asked me if I thought you good looking.'

'What did you say?'

'If I remember rightly—and I may have got a word or two wrong—I think I said something about every beetle being a beauty to its mother.'

He threw back his head and laughed.

She took a sip of her coffee. And another sip.

'Well, aren't you going to ask me?' he said a few minutes later. 'I asked you, after all.'

'Ask you what?' she said with feigned casualness.

'What I told her.'

'It's nothing to do with me.' She put her cup to her lips again.

'Well, I'm gonna tell you anyway. I said I liked you very much, but that nothing can compare with Conchita's enchiladas.'

She looked around for something to throw at him, but he'd moved too fast.

'Barbecue tonight it is, then. See you later,' he called

over his shoulder and went through the open doorway and headed for his den. 'Whoa! Slow down, Carey!' she heard him exclaim. 'You almost knocked me over.'

'I'm starving,' Carey said, hurrying out on to the terrace and sitting down opposite Leigh. 'I overslept. Conchita's getting my breakfast.'

'And good morning to you, too.'

'What you said.' She giggled.

'Here, let me pour you some orange juice.'

Carey watched as Leigh filled her glass with juice.

'I'm kinda surprised you're not yet married, Leigh,' she said, picking up her glass. 'You'd be an okay mom, I guess. You're bossy enough for the part.'

Leigh looked at her in surprise. 'Where did that come from?'

'I was just thinking. You've been in America for ages so you must've fallen in love with someone. What happened?'

The face of Carey's father swam into Leigh's mind: his strong jaw; the way his lazy smile made her toes curl; the laughter lines in the corners of his deep blue eyes; the warmth in his expression when he looked at her.

She met Carey's gaze. Carey's blue eyes seemed to be telling her that she knew something about her that she didn't want to face.

'Well?' Carey prompted.

'I suppose I cook for them too soon after meeting them, so things never get very far,' she said with a smile.

With a knowing smirk, Carey picked up her knife and fork and started on the breakfast that Conchita had just put in front of her.

Leigh shook herself.

First of all, she'd imagined that she was being watched by someone, but there'd been no one there. Now she was in danger of crediting Carey with supernatural powers. How was it Carey had described her—loopy?

LEIGH TOOK her own car and drove them into Beverly Hills, where she managed to find a parking space that wasn't too far from the manicurist's.

To her great delight, the first person she saw when she and Carey walked into the nail bar was Fran. Kim-Ly had just finished doing Fran's nails, and Fran was standing up, preparing to leave.

Instead of going home, Fran sat back down to chat, and while Leigh had her nails done, Fran kept Carey entertained with amusing anecdotes of the students she was teaching and their strange pottery creations. Leigh noted with amusement that 'amazing' was taking the place of 'gross', and fast becoming Carey's word of the moment.

When it was Carey's turn for her manicure, and she was absorbed in discussing the problems of school with Kim-Ly, who had a daughter of the same age, Fran started to badger Leigh for information about her and Matt.

She remarked on the happiness Leigh was exuding, and how perfect she and Matt had looked together, and she kept pressing for confirmation from Leigh that there was, indeed, a connection between Matt and the radiant glow on Leigh's face.

There wasn't, Leigh told her more than once, and there never would be—not someone like him with someone like her. But Fran was reluctant to go along with the 'there never would be' part of her answer.

Thank Heavens, Leigh thought with relief when Carey interrupted them, walking stiffly up to them, proudly displaying her newly painted pink fingernails and pointing happily to her equally pink toenails.

She and Carey said goodbye to Fran, and headed off to trawl through the hundred or so boutiques in the three famous tree-lined blocks between the Wilshire and Santa Monica Boulevards.

Later that evening, while Leigh, Matt and Carey were sitting in the spotlit garden after their barbecue, Carey told her father at great length how amazing she thought Fran.

He'd liked Fran and Jim, too, he said, and he suggested that he invite them to a restaurant one evening. When Carey and Leigh instantly jumped at the idea, he promised that he'd get on to it the next day.

THE FOLLOWING SATURDAY, Armando drove them to Santa Monica to meet up with Fran and Jim for dinner at Chez Jay.

'I'm really looking forward to seeing them again. Thank you for suggesting this, Matt.' Leigh smiled at him gratefully above Carey's head.

'My pleasure. I must say, I'm surprised that Van didn't wanna join us,' he said. 'I thought he'd jump at being included. Especially as it's a while since we've had dinner together. But he said he'd already made plans that he couldn't get out of.'

'He seems to have been really busy for the past couple of weeks or so, from what Conchita's said,' Leigh remarked.

"So I understand. She told me that he's been out more than he's been in. I'm not quite sure what he's doing, but he'll tell me in his own good time, and I'm happy to leave it till then. I trust him completely.'

'I'm glad he didn't come. I don't like him,' Carey said bluntly.

Matt glanced down at her, but didn't say anything.

The restaurant came in sight, and they saw that Fran and Jim had drawn up just ahead of them. After they'd enthusiastically greeted each other, they went into the restaurant, where they were shown to a booth.

When they'd finished ordering their cocktails and a Coca-Cola for Carey, who, Leigh realised in amusement, was in full rebellion against her mother's ban on fizzy drinks, Matt leaned back and smiled in contentment across the table at Leigh.

Catching his daughter watching him intently, he widened his smile to include her.

'I like it in here 'cos it's dark and people can't see us,' Carey said, looking around.

'That's one of the reasons for choosing this restaurant,' Matt said. 'I remembered you saying you didn't like people staring at us all the time. I figured that if they couldn't see us, they wouldn't stare.'

Carey beamed at him.

'How's the merger coming along, Matt, or rather the takeover?' Jim asked. 'Is everything going according to plan?'

Matt turned his attention to Jim. 'Indeed it is. It looks as if we'll be signing on the deal next week. It's a relief, I can tell you—it feels as if it's been a long ride. The legal team had an almost impossible task, but they did good—the whole team did good, in fact, and we're nearly at home base. It's possible we might even sign the contracts on Monday.'

'Monday!' Leigh exclaimed. 'So soon!'

'Yup. The last few weeks seem to have flown by, and it could well be Monday. I was going to suggest that you and Carey stayed at home on Monday, so that you'll be there if I come back with something to celebrate. To be honest, I can't take credit for that idea—it was Van's.'

'That's great news, Matt,' Jim said. 'It must be quite a weight off your mind.'

'And further good news is that Tom, my secretary, phoned this afternoon to say that his mother has made an amazing recovery, and he expects to be back next week. I forgot to tell you that, Leigh.'

Tom would be back within a week!

Leigh felt cold all over. She struggled to return Matt's smile, and it was a huge relief when he and Jim moved on to the project that Jim was working on, which didn't require her participation.

When Tom returned, Matt wouldn't need her for secretarial work. And when the school holidays ended, which wasn't that far away, Carey would go back to her mother, so she wouldn't be needed to help with Carey, either.

It meant that there'd no longer be a job for her at Matt's.

She felt a huge rush of sadness at the thought of saying goodbye to Carey, and she glanced at the girl, whose fair head was close to Fran's as the two of them peered at Fran's Hawaiian bracelet. She'd grown very fond of Carey, and she'd miss her enormously.

And as for leaving Matt.

Her anguish at the thought of leaving Matt hit her with such force that it winded her.

She felt completely distraught.

Choked up with misery for the rest of the meal, she went through the motion of eating and chatting, hoping her voice didn't sound as strange to everyone else as it did to her, all the time desperately longing to be back in her room and able to give way to the grief that kept threatening to break out and overwhelm her.

Finally, the seemingly never-ending meal came to an end, and they said goodbye to Fran and Jim.

'What a real good evening that was,' Matt remarked cheerfully as Armando drove the car along Santa Monica Boulevard. 'We must see them again before too long. I meet too few real people in my profession, and those guys are genuine and easy to get along with. You like them, too, Carey, don't you?'

Silence.

Leigh glanced down at Carey, who sat between them.

'She's fast asleep, Matt. We'd best not talk in case we disturb her,' Leigh whispered.

With the hard lump in her throat making it difficult to breathe, and almost impossible to talk, she was glad of an excuse not to have to try to speak, and she gazed out at the illuminated streets, longing for the moment when she'd be on her own and able to give way to her anguish.

When they reached the house, Carey yawned a good-night and wandered off to her bedroom.

'How about a nightcap?' Matt asked, turning to Leigh. 'It's been a lovely evening and I wouldn't mind prolonging it.'

'I'm sorry—I've got a headache,' she said quickly.

He took a step towards her, concern on his face, but she turned and half-ran along the corridor.

If only things could go back to the way they'd been before she met Matt, she cried out in herself. Life had been so simple then.

She'd been carefree and out for some fun, not weighted down by unwanted emotion. Oh, if only she'd never met him! If she hadn't, she wouldn't now be feeling more wretched than she'd ever felt before.

Tears were falling down her cheeks before she'd even reached her bedroom.

16

The day she'd been dreading arrived. Monday. The day that might be the start of her last week working for Matt.

Somehow she'd got through the long Sunday without anyone picking up on her misery. This was mainly because Matt had been tied up in his study for most of the day, Van had either been out or in discussion with Matt, and Carey had been with Maria from morning till evening.

When Sunday had finally drawn to a close, she'd gone to bed, drained and hoping to lose herself in sleep. But she'd hoped in vain. All night long, she'd tossed and turned, unable to stop herself from dwelling on what the Monday morning might bring.

There'd been a time when, if she was feeling low, all she had to do was fill her mind with thoughts of the good times she'd had in the past with her family and friends in England, and those memories would make her feel better.

But that time had passed. All England now meant to her was no Matt.

When Monday morning finally arrived, tired out and in

no mood for company, she stayed in her room until she was certain that Matt would have left for town.

When at last she left her room and headed for the veranda, she was relieved to hear screams of laughter coming from the garden. They told her that Carey must have already had breakfast and be playing with Maria, which meant that she wouldn't be forced into conversation for a while longer.

Conchita followed her out with the breakfast tray. 'Mr Matt get phone call at breakfast. He go change clothes and go out looking very smart man in dark suit and white shirt. Armando drive him. It big day for Mr Matt, I think,' she said, beaming in excitement.

'You could be right,' Leigh said, sitting down. 'Fingers crossed that it all goes well. Did Van go with him?'

Conchita shook her head. 'Mr Van not feeling well. He stay in house. He not want anyone disturb him—he sleeping.'

'Poor Van. He must be feeling pretty dire if he's not working. But he's not the only one staying at home today— Carey and I are, too. Not because anyone's ill, though. Van suggested to Matt that we stay at home today to be sure of being here at whatever time Matt gets back, just in case the deal's gone through.'

Conchita nodded vigorously. 'Is good idea.'

'It occurred to me that the girls might like a picnic lunch. Do you think you could do one for them?'

'Sí, Miss Leigh,' Conchita said, and she took herself back off to the kitchen.

Taking a hot cinnamon roll from the basket, Leigh spread it with butter and started eating for the sake of it, unable to taste a thing.

'Leigh!' she heard Carey scream.

She glanced across the grass and saw Carey running towards her. 'What are we doin' today?' Carey asked breathlessly, coming to a halt in front of the terrace.

'We're going to stay here all day. You and Maria can have the day to yourselves. You can swim if you want. Or watch a movie. Play pool, even. Whatever you want to do is fine by me—it's your choice. I think we all need a day of doing nothing. Don't you agree?'

'Cool!' Carey exclaimed. And she ran off, yelling to Maria to get some towels.

Leigh sighed in relief. Sitting under a parasol by the pool, watching the girls while they swam and played on the grass, was just about all she felt up to doing.

She finished her coffee, stood up, went into the house and got a book to read, and took it outside with her.

'You're getting quite a tan, Carey,' she told her when she reached the pool and found Carey and Maria sitting on the side, dangling their feet in the water. 'Don't forget the sun cream. Your mother would have a right to be mad if she thought you weren't protecting your skin, and that I wasn't doing anything about it.'

'She doesn't need a right to be mad—she's always mad. That's the way she is. When we've been swimming, we're gonna make a tent, aren't we, Maria? It'll be cool,' Carey said. 'Maria's got some sheets and towels with her. Conchita said she could.'

Cool was a vast improvement on gross, Leigh thought, and she pulled a lounger into the shade thrown out by the nearest large sun umbrella, settled herself on it and opened her book.

· · ·

CONCHITA's picnic hamper went down well, and the girls ate its contents among the trees behind the cabana.

Leigh was happy to let them get on with it by themselves, and she lay back on the lounger, her book unread, her lunch untouched on the table beside her, listening idly to their distant laughter.

She was absolutely longing for the day to be over, even though everything might still be up in the air when she went to bed, and the next day she might be faced with another similar day to struggle through.

But to her annoyance, the clock didn't seem to be moving.

A few feet away from her, the pool was sparkling in the afternoon sun. Maybe a swim would revive her, she thought in sudden hope.

But a sudden loud splashing, followed by wild screaming, told her that the hour after lunch of waiting to go into the water was up, and Maria and Carey had just jumped into the pool. She sat up, and resting on her elbows, watched them for a minute or two as they ducked each other under the water.

Or maybe not.

She didn't want to get in their way. She'd stay where she was.

Raising the back of the lounger slightly so that she could watch them more easily, she kept an eye on them until they climbed out of the pool and ran off, doing somersaults across the lawn.

Reaching over to the table, she picked up her book and started reading. A few pages into the book, she closed it—the last thing she wanted to read about was people declaring undying love for each other.

She returned the novel to the table, sat upright and looked towards the girls.

The top of the tent they'd made was visible just above the lavender bushes that lined the opposite side of the paved patio. The muffled sounds that were coming from that direction indicated that they were inside the tent.

Maybe she should go and check on them, see if they wanted a drink, or something else to eat.

She didn't move.

WHEN THE RAYS of the afternoon sun finally began to lengthen, she roused herself. It was time for the girls to pack their things away, for Maria to go to her apartment, and for her to go back to the house with Carey.

They'd need to shower and change for the evening.

Matt had booked a table at their favourite steakhouse to give them all a break from what had become his ongoing battle with the barbecue, he'd told them the day before. Tonight was going to be a treat for their stomachs. And just possibly, he'd added, a celebration, too.

She got up, walked across to the tent and peered inside.

'I'm sorry to break things up,' she said, 'but time's moving on and you need to think about getting ready, Carey. We're going out tonight, Maria.'

'Can Maria come, too?'

'Not this evening, I'm afraid, Carey. I've a feeling it might turn out to be a celebratory meal.'

'Not that boring Heartlands again,' Carey said with a groan. 'It's all Pop ever talks about these days.'

'Spot on. Except that it isn't boring. If he gets the company, it'll be a great achievement. So pick up your things, say goodbye to Maria, and get off to your room. You could wear your new pink dress. And as I see you've managed to get grass stains on your shorts, you'd better put them in the linen bin.'

'Like I said, you nag.' But Carey was smiling as she ran off.

Having stood and watched Maria run back to her parents' apartment above the block of garages, and then seen Carey disappear into the house, she leaned down to the girls' tent, and began to pull it apart.

When she'd done so, she scooped up the towels and sheets, carried them over to the cabana and dropped them into the linen bin, which was emptied daily.

Then she went through the trees to the place where the girls had eaten their lunch, and checked that they hadn't left any litter behind.

As she had almost finished, she thought she heard the sound of a car, and she stood listening. Could that be Matt, she wondered. But the car seemed to be going away from the house, not coming towards it, as the noise of the engine was gradually fading into the distance.

Sound was often deceptive, and it must have come from somewhere further away than it seemed, she thought, inwardly shrugging, and she continued with her tidying up.

When she'd picked up the possessions that the girls had left in the tent, on the grass and around the pool, she began to make her way back to the house, her arms full, her eyes on the paving stones in front of her. How many more times would she tread that path, she wondered.

Again she heard the sound of a car. But this time the car was definitely approaching the house. The engine shut down and she heard a door slam shut. And then shouting, followed by the sound of running feet.

She stopped in her tracks and stared towards the terrace.

A moment later, Matt ran through the open doorway and out across the lawn towards her, a broad smile on his face. His shirt was open at the neck. In one hand he carried his tie, and in the other, he was waving a bottle of champagne.

'We've done it, Leigh,' he shouted. 'We've done it. We've got Heartlands. We've signed.'

She dropped everything she'd been holding.

He reached her, pulled her close with his free arm and hugged her as if he'd never let her go. 'We've done it!' he cried again, and he brought his mouth hard down on hers.

Without thinking, she flung her arms around his neck and kissed him back, holding him tight.

'Oh, Leigh,' he said, burying his face in her hair. 'I'm real glad you're here.'

'Me, too. I'm so pleased for you, Matt.' And the tears she'd been holding back all day streamed down her cheeks.

He dropped his arm and wiped away her tears with his thumb. 'I understand. I feel emotional, too.' Laughing softly, he hugged her again.

'Come on,' he said, releasing her. 'Let's look for some champagne that hasn't been shaken around and toast the deal. Find Carey and tell her to come to the den. I'll ring Van's room and see if he's up to hauling himself out of bed and joining us.'

'I imagine Carey's already in the shower. She wouldn't want us to start without her, so why don't I quickly change first? I rather fancy being dressed to kill when we toast your success. I won't be long, I promise. I'll call for Carey on my way back in case she's still in her room. She'll have had long enough to get ready by then.'

. . .

SHE HAD the quickest of showers, hastily dried herself, and then hurried into her closet. She knew exactly what to wear as she had one dress that would be perfect for the occasion —the flame red dress she'd worn for so short a time on the night of Bob Lieberman's party.

She was determined to stop worrying about what happened when Tom returned and to make the most of the time she had left with Matt.

She'd feel a million dollars in the red dress, and that would help her to focus solely on enjoying the evening ahead.

She raised her arms and let the dress fall over her head.

For a moment, she stared at her reflection. Then she put her fingers to her lips, and touched the place where Matt had kissed her.

It hadn't meant anything, she told herself. It had been instinctive. He'd been wildly excited and happy, and she'd been there. She shouldn't attempt to make it what it wasn't, just because she'd love it to be that.

Then she slipped into her flame red heels, and went across to the house phone to call Carey and warn her that she was on the way.

There was no answer. Carey must already be with Matt, she thought, and she replaced the receiver and went out into the corridor.

As she passed Carey's room, she hesitated. There was an outside chance that Carey might not have heard the phone —she could have still been in the shower, for example, or drying her hair with a noisy drier.

Just in case Carey hadn't yet left her room, she knocked on the door, and called out, 'Are you ready, Carey?'

There was no answer so she continued to the den.

By the time she got there, Matt had put a white napkin

over the champagne cork and had stood the bottle in a silver ice bucket. He was bending slightly over the bucket as she went in, making sure that the ice covered the sides of the bottle.

He looked up at the sound of her footsteps, stopped what he was doing and straightened up.

'You look stunning, Leigh,' he said quietly. 'Real stunning.'

'Thank you.' She coloured slightly, and glanced quickly around the room.

'Where's Carey? I thought she'd be with you. I knocked on her door, but there wasn't an answer. And she didn't pick up the phone, either.'

'I haven't seen her yet. But you know Carey—she probably got involved with something, forgot the time, and then suddenly realised how late it was, jumped into the shower and didn't hear you. Or she could be in the kitchen, scrounging cakes from Conchita. I wouldn't put that past her.'

She laughed. 'That sounds par for the course with her. Except that she won't be with Conchita—Conchita went back to her apartment a while ago. There was no point in her staying on as we're out this evening, and Van made it clear this morning that he didn't want anything at all to eat today.'

'Well, as we've no idea how close to being ready Carey is, I suggest we start without her. She won't mind. And if she does, tough.'

He picked up the bottle and, with the napkin in position over the cork, uncoiled the wire that covered the cork. There was a loud pop as the cork sprang out and upwards. They looked up at the ceiling and laughed.

He poured the gushing champagne into two of the

glasses on the table, handed her one glass, took the other and raised it to her. 'To the future, Leigh.'

'To the future,' she echoed, and she took a sip of her drink. 'D'you think we should ring Van and see if he's feeling well enough to join us?'

'I had the same idea, but I couldn't get hold of him. I reckon he must be asleep.'

She frowned anxiously. 'He must be really bad to have been in his room all day. Perhaps we should check on him before we leave? He might need a doctor.'

He nodded. 'Yup, you're right. I'll do that. If I'm at all concerned, I'll get the doctor in, whatever he says. In the meantime, why don't we wait for Carey on the terrace—it's a lovely evening?'

He put his arm lightly around her shoulders, and together they strolled outside, taking their glasses with them, and sat down.

In front of them, the gardens shimmered gold in the dying light of the day.

'I love the evenings here,' Leigh said after a few moments of companionable silence. 'It's so peaceful.'

'Talking of peace, what on earth can Carey be up to?' He glanced back at the house.

'D'you want me to go and drag her from whatever it is?'

'Would you? The champagne will be flat soon, and we don't want to be late for the steakhouse. I made an early reservation because of Carey.'

'I won't be a minute.'

Leigh hurried along the corridor to Carey's bedroom, and knocked on the door. 'Come on now, Carey! You've had long enough to get ready.'

Silence.

She took a step back and stared at the door.

Maybe she'd fallen asleep. After all, she'd been playing hard all day and could easily be exhausted. She knocked again, and called Carey's name more loudly.

Still no answer. She put her ear to the door. There was no sound at all to be heard.

A chill of unease crept through her. She turned the handle, pushed the door open and went hesitantly into the room.

'Carey, are you ready?' she called.

An ominous silence hung in the air.

She glanced at the bed. Carey's new pink dress lay on it in a crumpled heap. On the bedside table, there was an opened can of Coca-Cola.

Her heart started pounding.

She ran to the bathroom and flung the door open—there was no one there and the shower was bone dry.

She lifted up the lid of the linen bin—Carey's shorts weren't in there, and nor were the rest of the clothes she'd worn that day. And they weren't on the bathroom floor. Nor were her towels. She ran back into the bedroom, but the shorts weren't on the floor there, either.

She pulled open the door of the walk-in closet, but the clothes that Carey had worn that day were nowhere to be seen.

There were a couple of hangers on the floor, and she automatically picked them up and hung them back on the trouser rail. And then she realised that Carey's favourite jeans weren't in their usual place, and nor were they anywhere else on the rails. She looked quickly around the closet—at least two T-shirts and a couple of jumpers were missing.

She caught her breath. Carey must have run away!

She ran back into the bathroom—her toothbrush and

toothpaste had gone, and her favourite sponge. The stainless steel rack that hung in the corner of the shower was empty, so she'd taken her soap and shampoo, too.

But why would she run away?

She ran to the inter-house phone and called Matt's study. After what seemed an eternity, Matt answered.

'Carey's not here, Matt,' she said rapidly, her words tumbling over each other. 'She's gone and so have some of her clothes. And her toothbrush.'

'She can't have gone.' His voice registered surprise, and then alarm. 'Are you sure?'

'I think so. Her favourite jeans have gone, but she doesn't seem to have changed out of her shorts. She's just taken some things and disappeared. She came back to get changed when Maria went home. That's it—Maria! Maria will know where Carey is! In fact, Carey might have gone across to her, and could be there now. She was pretty fed up with talk about Heartlands and she might have decided not to go out with us tonight after all. That could be it.'

'I'll ring Conchita.'

'It's her clothes being missing that's scaring me, Matt. I'm getting frightened.'

'Don't worry; we'll find her.' There was a click as he hung up.

When she got back to Matt, he was in the study, on the phone to Conchita.

'So you say you haven't seen her since lunchtime?' He paused to listen. 'I see. Would you? I'd be real grateful. Tell her she's not in any trouble, won't you? Yes, I know Maria's not a naughty girl. We just want to find out where Carey is, and Maria's the person most likely to know.' He hung up. 'Conchita hasn't seen her since lunch. She's sending Maria across.'

They hurried back out to the veranda and stared towards the path that Maria would come by.

A few moments later, they saw her running towards them. When she reached the veranda, she stopped sharply, and stood there, her face creased with worry.

Armando followed a short distance behind her.

Leigh stepped forward and smiled reassuringly. 'Don't worry, Maria; you haven't done anything wrong. We just wondered if you knew where Carey had gone. After all, you're her best friend and best friends tell each other everything.'

Maria looked from Leigh to Matt, bewildered. 'She hasn't gone anywhere. She's going out with you this evening.'

'You're absolutely sure she didn't mention any other plans?' Matt asked. 'Think carefully, honey. Whatever it is, you won't get into trouble.'

Maria's frown deepened, and she shook her head. 'She just say she was looking forward to having a steak that was properly cooked for a change. She say you're rotten at barbecuing. That's what she said.'

Matt nodded. 'That's fine, Maria. Some wires have obviously got crossed somewhere. We'll sort it out. You go back home with your father now.'

'She's clearly telling the truth,' Leigh said as Maria and Armando went back across the grass to their apartment.

'I know.' He glanced back at the house. 'While I hate to bother Van when he's unwell, he might have some ideas. I know it's hard to see Carey confiding in him, but it's worth a try. I'm gonna have a word with him.'

'And I'll check the gym and the indoor pool in case she's there and has lost track of the time. It's easily done. Or even had an accident and knocked herself out.'

Before she could reach the gym, she heard the sound of feet behind her, running towards her.

She stopped and turned round.

'He's not there, Leigh,' Matt said, panting. 'And he's not been there for quite a while—his bed's stone cold. What's more, some of his things are missing. I think he's gone, too.'

She gasped and put her hand to her mouth.

'You carry on and check the gym,' he went on, 'and I'll go back to the study and call Cybill. Carey could've gone there. It's a long shot, but she just might have told Cybill she was leaving. And possibly even elicited Van's help to do so.'

When she'd checked the indoor pool and gym, and found both of them empty, she ran back to Matt's study.

The receiver was in his hand. 'Cybill was out,' he told her. 'Her maid told me where she was, and I rang the place. They're getting her now. Ah, Cybill,' he said, and he turned slightly away from Leigh. 'Am I glad I caught you! To cut to the quick, do you know where Carey could be—she seems to have vanished?'

Leigh went closer to him.

He listened for a moment, glanced back at Leigh and shook his head. 'Okay, then. And you'll let me know if she gets in touch with you.' He paused. 'Good idea. And the first to hear something will call the other.' He replaced the phone.

'I take it she hasn't heard from Carey,' Leigh said, her face pale.

'Not a word. She's in a cocktail bar somewhere with friends. But she's going to go straight home in case Carey turns up.'

'If it wasn't for the can of Coke on her bedside table and her dress on the bed, I'd think Carey hadn't been back to her room since I last saw her. But she must've picked up the drink after getting back to the house—they had lemonade with their lunch—and she must have got out her dress for tonight. I can't stop thinking about a car I thought I heard. It was just before you got home.'

'I'm calling the police,' he said, and he picked up the phone again. 'I should've done so sooner.'

17

'The police are on their way,' Matt said. 'But I can't stand around doing nothing while we wait for them to get here. I'm going back to Van's room—they may've dropped something when they took him.'

She drew in her breath in alarm. 'So you think they've both been kidnapped?'

'It's the only thing that makes sense. Van must've heard Carey scream or seen something suspicious and gone to investigate.'

'Oh, Matt, you don't think ...? No; he wouldn't.'

'Think what?'

She stared at him, and her words fell out in a rush. 'You don't think Van could have taken her? Whoever took her knew what clothes to take. Yes, Van might have heard her scream, gone to help her and got caught, but the kidnappers wouldn't have had time to go to his room and pack his things. And some of his clothes are missing, too, you said.' She shook her head. 'It doesn't make sense, though, that Van, of all people, would do such a thing. He's been your friend for years. I must be wrong.'

Wordlessly, they stared at each other.

Then Matt sprang into action. 'Nothing's ruled out at this stage. While we wait for the cops, you take a closer look at Van's bedroom, and I'll go through his office—there might be something there.'

'THERE'S no mess in his room. He obviously had time to pack. And he's taken a lot. More than it looks at first glance. I'd say that he's taken just about anything he'd want to keep,' Leigh told Matt when she joined him in Van's office.

She glanced around the office. 'And it looks as if he's taken a lot from here, too. The stuff that's left behind is neatly placed on the shelves, like it was in his closet, which means he wasn't taken by surprise. He'll have been the person who did the packing.' She paused. 'Have you found anything yet?'

'Not a thing. I phoned Conchita to ask what time she last saw Van, but she's not seen him at all today. He called her this morning and said he was ill and wanted to be left to sleep all day. He didn't want anyone to disturb him, and he didn't want lunch.'

'Yes, that's what she told me.'

'While I was talking to her, Armando went and unlocked Van's garage and found his Buick missing. I'm afraid you're right, Leigh—he seems to have left under his own steam, presumably with Carey.' His voice broke. 'I can't even bear to think it, but they could be miles away by now.'

She put her hand lightly on his arm. 'But why would he do such a terrible thing?'

'It'll be about money. I'll be sent a ransom demand, you can bet,' Matt said. He put his hand to his head. 'God, this waiting's awful!'

'Perhaps there's a clue somewhere here as to where they've gone.' She gave a sudden start. 'I've just had a thought! I wonder if this has got anything to do with Italy. Van said something about Cybill making a film deal with an Italian studio. I got the impression he was helping her. It means he must have some contacts over there. You don't think he could be taking Carey to Italy, do you?'

'I suppose he could,' he said slowly, 'but it's unlikely. He'd need her passport for a start, and Cybill would hardly have given Carey her passport just to come here.'

'I'd forgotten the passport thing. No, it won't be that, then.' She looked around. 'Well, shall we have another look at everything here while we're waiting?'

'I suppose it'd be something to do.'

'Right. You've obviously been through the desk drawers, and not found anything, but you'll have looked very quickly, Matt, and it might be an idea to double-check. I can begin on the cabinets.'

'It's as good a plan as any. I don't think I've ever felt so helpless, Leigh,' he said in despair.

She put her arms around him and hugged him. 'The police will find her. You'll see. But the waiting will be easier if we keep busy.'

She dropped her arms, moved across to the cabinets, pulled out the top drawer of the cabinet closest to her, took out the contents and started carefully checking the items one by one.

In the distance, they heard the shrill whine of police sirens.

'Thank God; they're almost here.' Matt's voice shook with relief. 'Will you let them in while I finish going through his desk drawer? It's the most likely place to find something.'

Leigh didn't move.

'Leigh. The police will need to be let in. But I'll go if you want.'

Still she didn't move. She was staring down at a torn scrap of paper that she'd carefully removed from the inside of a notebook she'd taken from the top cabinet drawer.

The piece of paper looked as if it had come from a leaflet. The leaflet must have been tucked into the notebook, she realised, and got caught in the binding. When Van took it out, the edge had torn off and stayed trapped. It was such a narrow strip of paper that Van probably hadn't even noticed.

'What've you found?' Matt moved quickly to her side.

She held up the torn strip. 'You can see the first word of each sentence, but that's all. I've no idea what it's about as it isn't in English. I think it's in Spanish. The notebook caught my eye as it was slightly out of line, and looked as if Van might've been handling it recently.'

She handed the piece of paper to Matt.

'I've no idea if it's significant,' she added, 'but it might be an idea to know what the leaflet's about. How's your Spanish, or shall we ask Conchita?'

He frowned at it for a moment, and then his face cleared. 'I know what this is,' he cried in sudden excitement. 'I've seen documents like this before. It's from a Mexican Auto Insurance document. If you have a car accident in Mexico, you've gotta have the document with you. If you don't, they put you in jail. Van and I used to go to Mexico a lot as he's got folk there. It's not Italy he's heading for—he's gone south to Mexico.'

The roar of sirens filled the drive.

'If he's still on the San Diego Freeway the police should be able to catch him. But it depends on when he left. It's about three hours from here to Tijuana, so if he left as long as three hours ago, he could be close to the border by now, or even already be in Mexico if he didn't hit traffic. I sure hope he isn't. If he's crossed the border, it'll be all but impossible to find him. What time did you last see Carey?'

'Late afternoon—about half an hour before you got back.' She gave a sudden exclamation. 'I bet it was Van's car that was driving away!'

'How long was that before I got home?'

'About fifteen minutes, I'd say.'

Car doors slammed outside.

'And you were in your room for about thirty minutes, Leigh. Then we talked while we waited for Carey, and then we looked for her—that's another twenty minutes or so. So they'd left about an hour before we found she was missing.'

'Don't forget you talked to Conchita.'

'That's right. And after that, we searched some more in the house. That means they'll be well on the way to the border by now, but probably not quite there. If only we'd realised sooner where they'd be heading.'

'I'm sure it's not too late, Matt. The police are here. They've got helicopters. They'll get him.'

The doorbell rang.

18

Van took his eyes fleetingly off the road and glanced across at Carey. She was still asleep.

But it wouldn't be a deep sleep—the effects of the sleeping draught must have virtually worn off, and she'd wake up easily enough when he wanted her to. When she did wake up, she'd be disorientated and unable to remember anything.

And she'd be highly suggestible.

Seeing her doing for once what he'd told her to do was going to be quite a novelty, and one he looked forward to. She'd be completely unrecognisable from that mouthy brat he'd had to put up with for so long.

For far too long.

Cybill Harding should have shut her daughter up as soon as she started cheeking her betters. But did she? No! Being permanently absorbed in herself, Cybill had been far too lazy and egocentric to exercise any control over the girl, and had sat back and done nothing in the face of Carey's increasing rudeness.

Rich kids needed tough discipline, and until he got his

money and dumped Carey, that was what she was going to get.

And what a surprise for her it'd be. For if Cybill Harding had been lax with her spoilt daughter, the saintly Leigh Carter had been even worse!

All that smiling and sucking up to the girl, just to get to the father!

Well, it was all going to have been in vain.

The horror of his daughter being snatched from under the perfect Miss Carter's eyes was bound to attach itself to the woman, and in future, every time that Matt Hunter looked at that simpering secretary, he'd remember what had happened to Carey, and he'd blame Miss Carter.

And she wouldn't seem quite so perfect any longer.

Anything that had been developing between them would have come to a swift and permanent halt the moment that Matt Hunter found out that Carey had been taken while Leigh Carter had been sitting on her backside in the sun.

His lips curled into a smile of triumph. So far, everything had gone like clockwork. But he'd known it would—he'd planned it down to the very last detail.

As soon as he'd learned that Matt would be tied up all day with Heartlands, and that Armando would be with him, he'd known that his time had come.

A word or two in Matt's ear had ensured that Leigh and Carey would remain at the house all day, and he knew that in all likelihood Carey would play with Maria until late in the afternoon.

It meant that he'd been able to tuck the Mexican Auto Insurance form into the side pocket of the driver's door, and load the suitcases he'd already packed into the back of the car without any fear of being seen.

After that, he'd gone quickly to Carey's room, thrown a few of her things into a bag, and put the bag into the car next to his cases.

He'd then watched for Carey to return to the house, confident that she'd be by herself.

Leigh always got back to the house after Carey, as it was Leigh who picked up everything that had been left behind by Carey and Maria. Carey was far too self-important to clear up the mess that she and Maria had made.

All he'd had to do was step forward as Carey came into the house, two open cans of Coca-Cola in his hand, and explain that he'd just opened the second can by mistake and offer it to her. Of course she'd taken it. Cybill's ban on Coca-Cola meant that Carey drank it at every possible opportunity.

It had been a simple enough matter to follow her back to her room, wait outside for the drug he'd put into her can of Coke to take effect, and then carry her listless body to the car.

Given the amount of sleeping drug that he'd given her, he hadn't had much of a wait, which had been important as he wasn't sure at what time Matt would return.

All Carey had been able to do before she felt woozy was take her dress from the closet. Overcome by the need to sleep, she'd then sprawled out on her bed and closed her eyes.

Getting her limp body across to his car had been the most fraught part of the plan because there was an unavoidable element of the unknown, and a number of things could've gone wrong.

Conchita might have had a shorter siesta than usual, and Maria might have hung around outside their apartment for an inordinate amount of time after saying goodbye to

Carey. If so, either one of them could have seen him if he'd gone to the garage.

Carey might've left less of a mess than usual, and Leigh might've cleared up more quickly than he'd bargained upon. And, of course, Matt could have returned at any time.

If there'd been a hitch in Matt's plans for the day, he would almost certainly have returned earlier rather than later, and Armando might have reached the garage block before he'd had time to leave.

But in as far as he could, he'd prepared for every eventuality, and had come up with a story he'd be able to adjust according to whom he was speaking.

Basically, if challenged, he would've said that Carey was ill and he was taking her to the hospital as quickly as possible, and that Matt would be meeting them there.

He'd say that Leigh was packing some overnight things for Carey, and would follow him. And by the time they'd all compared notes, gone to the hospital, found no trace of him or Carey, and realised that something was amiss, he and Carey would have been far away.

But it had all gone without a hitch, and he'd left the house unseen and driven off, a sleeping Carey at his side.

Having made the necessary detour to the garage he'd rented secretly a few weeks earlier, he'd swiftly transferred Carey and their bags from his Buick to the used Chevy he'd bought. Then he'd locked the Buick in the garage, and driven off in the Chevy.

It had put them on the road to Mexico in a car with a full tank, that didn't draw attention to itself, with no one having the slightest idea where they were going and nor in what vehicle they'd be travelling.

If they tried to guess at his destination, there was a strong chance that they'd come up with Italy, and he'd be surprised if they didn't focus significant resources on the airport.

Getting a no-account Italian studio interested in signing Cybill for a three-film deal had been inspired.

He'd made sure of mentioning the Italian deal to Leigh, so that when they were trying to work out where he would go, Italy was bound to have come up as a possibility, and they were likely think he was helping Cybill take Carey to Italy without Matt's knowledge.

They'd reckon that Cybill wouldn't want Matt to know that she was taking Carey overseas, as he would be sure to fight tooth and nail for custody of the girl if he knew in advance of such a plan.

They'd obviously also wonder if Mexico might be his destination as he and Matt had stayed with his Mexican relatives on more than one occasion in the past. There was no way of preventing that, but he hoped that as they'd have more than one possible destination upon which to focus, it would divide their resources to his advantage.

And once they were in Mexico, Matt wouldn't have a hope in hell of finding him.

He smiled in quiet satisfaction.

How he would've loved to have been a fly on the wall when Cybill was told that Carey was missing! What a joy it was to know that it was his action that will have wiped that artificial smile off her plastic face.

It would certainly go some way towards rewarding him for years of pretending to admire Cybill, while all the time dripping into her ear the unpleasant comments Matt was supposed to have made about her. Flattering such a shallow, conceited woman may have been a long, tedious slog, but it had been worth it—Cybill had come to trust him.

She'd believed what he told her about Matt's negative

attitude towards her, and had stopped Carey from visiting him. As a result, he'd had the instant gratification of seeing his smug boss tear himself up, month after month, at not being able to see his daughter.

The grief that Carey's absence had caused Matt had been satisfying in as far as it went, but it was small fry compared with the anguish that Matt would be feeling at Carey's disappearance, an anguish that filled him with a sense of real achievement.

Persuading Cybill to send Carey to stay with Matt had been stage one of putting his master plan into action.

At first, she'd been reluctant to allow Matt the pleasure of seeing his daughter, but from the moment he'd pointed out that a rude, mouthy teenager was just the person to drive a wedge between Matt and Leigh, she hadn't been able to push Carey into the car fast enough.

The thought of her ex being happy in his private life as well as in his career had been too much for her, and her fervent hope had been that Carey would put her worst foot forward and show her father just how difficult and unpleasant she could be.

With Carey ensconced in a place from which he could easily snatch her, putting the rest of his plan into action had been like taking candy from a baby.

But he was after a lot more than candy—a whole lot more.

He was after payment for all the years he'd had to be so very grateful for the scraps that Matt had thrown from his table, so very humble before such largesse. And for having always had to be so praising of Matt's success, when in reality he, Van, was the one with the big talent.

Part of his payment was knowing the anguish he'd

caused, and would continue to cause. But it would also come in the form of money—lots of money.

He'd get ransom money from Matt, and then money from the kidnappers to whom he'd sell Carey after he'd collected from Matt.

If the kidnappers didn't want to follow him down the same path of asking for a ransom, a pretty young girl, blonde, as yet untouched by a man, would sell for a high price. Oh, yes; he intended to milk Carey for every dime he could get.

If Matt thought he was going to see his daughter again, he was very much mistaken.

And when Matt and his cronies went over what must have happened, they'd see his meticulous planning. And also the skilful way in which he'd cultivated a false image over so long a period, and they'd realise what a superb actor he was and what opportunities they'd wasted in not using him in A-grade films, and they'd be filled with regret.

That would be his final satisfaction.

Yes, he was going to get a whole lot more than just a little bit of candy.

He glanced across at Carey and started to laugh.

19

A few of the police officers climbed back into their cars and drove off. But a couple of police cars and three vans remained on Matt's drive.

Matt turned to the Beverly Hills Police Chief, who was standing next to him. 'I appreciate you coming here in person, Chief. It's helped a lot to know that you're personally involved.'

'Anything I can do, sir, you only have to say. The next few hours are going to be mighty hard on you, but you should try to relax, though I reckon that's easier said than done. Stay near the phone in case the kidnappers call.'

'You say kidnappers. You don't think Van's acting alone?'

'We've no idea at this stage whether he's on his own in this or not. Forensics may be able to help us with this when they've finished. In the meantime, our agents have set up everything in your office, and they'll listen in to both sides of any call, and advise you about your response. A liaising officer will also stay with you—he'll be always be close at hand, should you need him.'

Matt gestured his helplessness. 'I can't just sit and wait.

There must be something I can do.'

'There isn't, sir. You must leave everything to us—we know what we're doing. The FBI has a very high conviction rate for kidnapping, and most kidnappers get caught. Mr Attwood is not gonna be an exception, and nor is anyone else involved. But our priority is securing Carey's release.'

'Of course, it must be.'

'The advantage is on our side,' the Police Chief went on. 'We know who the kidnapper is, even though we don't know if he's acting alone, and we know where he's heading. But we don't know what he's driving. My guess is, the Buick's in a lock-up somewhere not far from here. He'll have swapped cars as soon as possible. But we'll get him nevertheless.'

Matt sighed in despair. Leigh moved closer to him, and he put his arm around her. 'I wish I could feel as confident,' he said. 'If he crosses into Mexico, we've lost him.'

'We're gonna do everything possible to see that doesn't happen. The helicopters are in the air as we speak. We've set up roadblocks, and alerted the border police. In case the Insurance Certificate is a red herring, we've circulated Carey's photo to airports in the region, and to all police stations in California and south as far as Mexico.'

'What about a hostage negotiator? Shouldn't you have one, just in case?'

'And we have one coming, sir. There's a highly skilled negotiator flying to Tijuana, as we still think that the border crossing there is the most likely destination. We've put more police on the Tijuana streets, and we've got more patrol cars out. We're on top of it, sir. You must be patient and try to relax.'

'I'll do my best. But you'll let us know the minute you hear anything, won't you?' He paused, and then added, 'No matter how awful.'

'You can count on it. By the way, we've told your ex-wife she must stay at home—there's a chance that Attwood might contact her, rather than you. We've a team of operatives on the way to her now, and I'm off to join them. You've got my personal number. Don't hesitate to contact me if you think of anything else, however unimportant it might seem. But, hopefully, there'll be good news very soon.'

He went over to his car, got into the back seat and his driver headed out through the gates.

Leigh glanced up at the windows above the garage block. Maria was leaning out, watching the chief's car as it drove off.

She looked down at Leigh and their eyes met. Maria's eyes accused her. Then she stepped back into her room, pulled the window closed and disappeared.

'Maria blames me,' she said turning back to Matt. 'And I blame myself, too. Carey went missing when I was looking after her.'

'She's just upset; we all are. It's not your fault—Van's planned this meticulously. And he could do that because I trusted him completely. It makes it my fault, rather than anyone else's. In fact, it's thanks to you that we've a pretty good idea where he's heading, and that we found out so quickly. I'm always gonna be grateful to you for that.' He tightened his arm around her. 'Come on; let's go in.'

Conchita was hovering in the entrance hall, her eyes red-rimmed.

'We'll have coffee in the den, Conchita. And will you see what the operatives want?' Matt said. 'Much as I could use something stronger than that, I need to keep a clear head. After that, you must go home and be with Maria. I imagine she's in a real state. We'll let you know as soon as we hear anything.'

His arm still around Leigh, they went along the corridor to the den and sat down together on the sofa.

Matt leaned back, his arm loosely around Leigh's shoulders. 'What I'd really like to do is fly to Mexico to try and stop the car from crossing the border. But I'd be too late. Even with heavy traffic, they're bound to be there by now.'

'But how will Van get Carey into Mexico? Cybill's got Carey's passport, hasn't she?'

'She doesn't need a passport—she's a minor. All he needs is a copy of her birth certificate. He could have easily gotten that—he used to visit Cybill. He thought I didn't know, but I did. It was none of my business, though—it was up to him what he did when he wasn't working. To be honest, I rather thought he might be keen on her.'

'I once wondered that, but I changed my mind.'

He nodded. 'And I'm now rethinking it. Taking Carey won't have been a spur of the moment thing, and heaven knows how long this has been in the planning. It's beginning to look as if he was using Cybill all the time.'

He paused. 'Of course, he might not cross the border at Tijuana,' he said, looking at Leigh in alarm. 'He could've gone further along the border to an illegal crossing point. I hope the police have thought of that.'

'I'm certain they have, Matt. But I bet the FBI catches him long before then. It's a shame if they're right about him changing cars, but I expect that's what he did. His Buick was far too distinctive, and you know his licence number.'

'What I don't get is why he'd do such a thing,' Matt said, shaking his head in bewilderment. 'If he needed money, I would've given it to him. He must've known that. I just don't understand it.' He looked around the room, his gaze coming to rest on the telephone on the side table next to the sofa. 'I never thought I'd feel sorry for Cybill, but I do. I wonder how she's coping. At least I've got you.' He tightened his arm around her. 'I can't imagine how I'd have got through this without you.'

'You don't have to imagine it, Matt—I'm here with you.'

He looked down into her face. 'Yes, you are,' he said quietly. 'And I'm mighty thankful for it.'

There was a sound on the opposite side of the room, and they looked quickly at the door as Conchita came in with a large tray. Next to a pot of coffee there were two tacos and a bowl of refried beans.

'You not have dinner. You must eat.' She put down the tray, pulled a handkerchief out of her apron pocket and turned away. Applying the handkerchief to her eyes, she went out sniffing loudly.

Leigh handed a taco to Matt. The phone rang.

He dropped the taco.

An FBI agent materialised at his side. He indicated that the team was ready and that Matt should answer the phone.

With a quick glance at Leigh, he turned towards the side table, picked up the receiver and listened.

Her heart beat loudly for what felt like the longest moment in her life.

Then he gasped, and turned to her. 'She's safe, Leigh. She's safe. They've found them. Van's in custody. And she's not been hurt. What a relief! They said she's drowsy, but she's sufficiently awake to make her wishes known. She wants to come home and they're flying her back this evening.' His voice broke.

He let the receiver fall, put his face in his hands and wept.

Leigh leaned forward, wrapped her arms around him, and sat very still, tears running down her cheeks.

20

Leigh stepped out on to the veranda into the scented late-morning air, and looked around.

The world had never looked more beautiful. The birds were singing, the cloudless sky was a clear cerulean blue, the gardens were verdant green in the radiance of the sun, and the pool glistened like sparkling champagne.

Tom's imminent return was far from her thoughts. All she could think was that Carey was safely back at home with them.

Matt was already sitting on the veranda, and she went across and sat down next to him.

'You must be exhausted,' he said. 'I certainly am. What a day it was yesterday. From the heights of excitement about the deal going through, to the depths of despair. I don't think I've ever been as scared as I was. And then to see Carey again, after all our fears. What a moment! I doubt you slept any more than I did when you finally got to bed.'

'I didn't, and I should feel tired, but I don't. I just feel so happy, and so relieved. And also a bit nervous about what might have happened, even though it didn't. It's frightening how close we came to losing Carey. After all, it was only a matter of luck they caught Van.'

'Don't I know it! If that drunk hadn't driven into him in Tijuana, and caused the door to jam, he would've taken Carey and fled from the car before the police could get there. But he couldn't open the door. And because he'd left his insurance form in the Buick, he was arrested for not having it with him. The Mexican police had his details, so they knew to be on the lookout for him, and the second they saw his face, the game was up.'

'We ought to frame the bit of the document we found in his notebook. First it showed us where he was going, and then it helped the police to catch him when he got there.'

He laughed. 'Good idea. But I think we'll let the dust settle first.'

'I can't wait for Carey to wake up,' Leigh said happily.

'Nor me. But you and I have got some talking to do, and it might be better to do it while she's still asleep.' He turned to face her. 'Tom phoned, and he'll be back tomorrow evening,' he said evenly.

She felt the blood drain from her face.

'But I don't want you going anywhere,' he added quietly. 'You belong here with me, Leigh. And I don't mean as an agency temp.'

'What are you saying, Matt?' She caught her breath at the expression in his eyes, and a look of wonder spread across her face. Each moved towards the other.

'I trust I'm not interrupting anything important.'

At the sound of a husky voice behind them, they spun round.

A tall slim woman stood in the open doorway, one arm casually on her hip, the other gracefully stretching up and resting lightly against the wall. She held the position for a moment, her flawless body displayed to perfection, and then moved forward.

'Cybill!' Matt exclaimed, rising to his feet. 'Full marks for the entrance. Nobody can make an entrance quite like you. I take it Conchita let you in. But forgive me—it must have escaped my memory, but I don't recall inviting you.'

Ignoring her ex-husband, Cybill Harding glided across the terrace to their table.

In one glance, Leigh took in the smooth chignon into which the actress's long blonde hair had been skilfully wound, the narrowed violet eyes that were fringed by long dark lashes, the red gash of a mouth and the slender neck which rose dramatically from a black sheath dress that would have been more suitable for a dinner party than to wear on a bright sunny morning.

Matt's ex-wife was the epitome of sleek sophistication, she thought, cringing as she glanced down at her crumpled yellow cotton dress.

'Leigh, allow me to introduce you to Cybill, my ex. I expect you've heard about Leigh from Van, Cybill, since we know you've been in touch with each other. She's standing in for Tom while he's in Chicago, as you'll already know.'

'I sure do.' She lifted a perfectly sculpted eyebrow and acknowledged Leigh with a slight inclination of her head. Her expression was one of open disdain.

She may be beautiful, Leigh thought, but she was cold. It was no wonder that Carey had said that her parents were very different from each other. The wonder was that they'd ever got together in the first place.

'I've come to check that Carey is well, and to take her back home with me, where I know she'll be safe.'

'Sorry, Cybill, but that doesn't hold water as a reason for

you being here. When I phoned you last night, I told you that Carey was fine, but sleepy, and so did the police. Did you really crawl out of bed at what is an unheard-of hour for you, just to see that for yourself? I don't think so. As for taking Carey back with you—you know I would've driven her back if you'd insisted.'

'I know that, darling. But I'm a creature of impulse.' She gave a silvery laugh. 'When I woke up, I just knew I had to see Carey for myself, to know for sure that she was unharmed. It was a spur of the moment decision to come this morning.'

Leigh glanced at Cybill Harding's immaculate grooming and artfully chosen outfit, set off to perfection with its matching accessories.

'It must have been a very long moment,' she observed cuttingly.

Matt choked on a cough.

The look Cybill gave Leigh was a mixture of icy contempt and naked dislike. Turning back to Matt, she treated him to a practised smile, into which she'd injected an apologetic note. Silly little me, but I'm an impulsive mother, her deprecatory smile managed to insinuate.

'And maternal concern is really the only thing that brought you here this early?' Matt asked, his voice full of disbelief.

Leigh noticed a momentary loss of confidence in Cybill, but she seemed to recover her equilibrium.

'How clever of you, darling,' Cybill purred. 'Actually, I do have another reason for coming. I have some good news and I wanted to tell it to you in person.' Her studied smile didn't quite reach up to her eyes, Leigh noticed. 'But we'll need champagne.'

She extended a manicured hand in the direction of the den.

'Just tell us your news, Cybill. If we agree that it's good, we'll open a bottle, toast your news and then you can leave. It'll give us two lots of good news to toast—what happened yesterday rather interrupted us celebrating my deal and we can toast that, too.'

She inclined her head. 'As you wish.'

'As for Carey, though,' he added. 'Upon reflection, I think we'll hang on to her for another couple of days, and then bring her back.'

Cybill opened her mouth to speak.

Matt held up his hand to stop her. 'She could suffer from delayed shock, and she needs to be given time to settle down again. Relaxing with Maria will help her do that. Also, I don't want her primarily associating this house with a frightening experience, which she might do if you took her back with you today.'

She hesitated. 'Oh, all right. Because I'm in a good mood, I'll agree.'

'What's put you in this good mood, then?' he asked. 'Why don't you sit down and tell us?'

Remaining standing, Cybill cleared her throat. 'I've agreed to a three-film contract with La Dolce Vita Studios near Milan. We were finalising matters when you called yesterday. Now that Carey's been found, I can go ahead and sign the contract. A time's been arranged for tomorrow morning. So, I've a three-film contract—that's my good news.'

Matt stared hard at her. 'You look nervous under all that make-up. What aren't you telling me?'

Cybill fixed her eyes defiantly on Matt. 'That I'm moving to Italy, and I'm taking Carey with me. You'll have to manage without her for the next few years, or go to Italy if you want to see her.'

'You're doing what, Mom?' Carey's voice came from behind Cybill.

All eyes focused on Carey.

She stood in the doorway in pyjamas, her face as white as a sheet.

21

The first person to move was Carey. She ran to her father, tucked her hand in his and faced her mother defiantly.

'You can go where you want; I'm staying here. And even if you weren't going to rotten ol' Italy, I'd still want to stay here. I wanna live with Dad.'

'You heard what Carey said, Cybill. She wants to live with me. As there's nothing I'd like better, I'll fight you every inch of the way to make that happen.'

'And you'll lose. Courts favour the mother, as you well know from past experience.' Cybill's lip curled.

Carey dropped her father's hand and stepped forward. 'But *I* won't lose!'

'Keep out of this, Carey. You don't know what you're talking about,' Cybill snapped.

'No, I won't. It's about me, this is. You're trying to get back at Dad by taking me somewhere I don't wanna go. And I bet you don't either. And I'm not going.'

'You're twelve and you'll do what I say. I'm your mother.'

'Not for long,' Carey said, her face mutinous. 'I'm gonna

go to court—I'm divorcing you. Some kid in Florida called Gregory divorced his parents, and I'm divorcing you. You don't love me. You don't use someone to get back at someone else if you love them. Dad loves me and I love Dad, and I'm staying with him.'

Cybill went white with rage. 'That's what you think, but you're wrong. As your father well knows, Carey, but you obviously don't, the courts would never give a child of your age to your father, not when he's away for weeks at a time, and not when I'm not guilty of anything. So, to use words I've heard often enough from you, tough luck—you're staying with me.'

'Dad being away won't be a problem,' Carey said, but she suddenly sounded less than convinced, Leigh noticed.

Leaning closer to Matt, Carey glanced at Leigh in despair. Then her face rapidly brightened, and she straightened up.

'That's not a problem,' she announced triumphantly. 'Pop's marrying Leigh. I'm gonna have a step-mom. It'll be wicked.'

A loud silence fell on to the veranda.

Then Matt moved nearer to Leigh, and put his arm around her shoulder.

'What with Heartlands and the fright Van gave us yesterday,' he said calmly, 'I've not yet had time to tell you, but Carey's right, Cybill. Leigh has become much more than a secretary to me.'

His arm tightened around Leigh's shoulder.

'You're lying, both of you,' Cybill said coldly. 'You'd never marry a nobody like her.' She looked at Leigh in scorn.

'Yes, he would,' Carey cut in, her voice indignant. 'She's real nice. Any dork can see that Pop loves Leigh and she loves him. Of course, they're gonna get married.'

'From the moment I met Leigh, I knew she was the woman I wanted to be with for the rest of my life,' Matt said, his voice filled with emotion.

Leigh's heart missed a beat.

'And Leigh felt the same, didn't you, Leigh?' he said, his voice caressing her. With his index finger, he turned her face to look up into his.

Laughter danced in the eyes that stared into hers.

'How moving this all is,' Cybill said, acidly. 'How simply too moving. It could even be the script of a movie. Come to think of it, darling, I think it was. But beautifully delivered, anyway. You always did know how to sell a line.'

Leigh stared up at Matt in bewilderment. She couldn't believe he'd gone along with what Carey had said. But he pulled her closer to him, his hand on her arm pressuring silence.

'I've uttered a lot of clichés in my career, so why stop now, when a cliché describes exactly how I feel?' he carried on, gazing with open adoration at Leigh. 'By agreeing to become my wife, Leigh has made me the happiest man alive. And as you can tell, Cybill, Carey, too, is delighted that Leigh is joining the family.'

He turned and looked at Carey, his expression unfathomable.

She stared innocently up at him, and then allowed her face to break into a saintly smile.

He gave a slight shake of his head, and turned away to look back at Leigh. Their eyes met. A faint smile played around his lips, and she felt herself going red.

'But I think we can now stop talking about Leigh as if she isn't here,' Matt said. 'Suffice it to say, you'll not be going to Italy, Carey, other than to visit your mother if she chooses to go alone. And you won't need to take her to court, either.'

'That's what you think,' Cybill retorted, white with anger.

'That's what I know. If you attempt to take Carey with you, I'll fight you, and I'll win. Carey's a lot older now. The courts will take a dim view of anything that disrupts her education, and they'd hardly approve of her being taken to a country, at her age, where she doesn't speak the language, not when she has a father and step-mother at home, wanting to look after her.'

'She can learn Italian,' Cybill snapped.

'And here's something else for you to think about, Cybill. Deep down, you don't really want to live in Italy. You don't speak the language any more than Carey does. And you're American through and through. You love the glamour and glitz of Hollywood. It's where you belong. I can't see you living on your own in Italy, miles away from the people with whom you've something in common. That's not you, Cybill —you're a party girl. You wanna go out and have fun— Hollywood-type fun.'

Cybill stared at Matt, uncertainty flickering in her eyes. 'But I've got a career ahead of me in Italy,' she said at last. 'What have I got here?'

Matt gave her a half-smile. 'A good part in a movie. I'm not bribing you for Carey—I don't have to do that to get her. I'm offering you an olive branch for the sake of our daughter. I believe it's better for her to have both her parents in her life.'

Cybill looked at him, with sudden hope. 'What're you saying, Matt? That you'll give me a role in a film?'

'That's right. I reckon I must take some of the blame for the animosity between us. I was too busy developing my acting career and the business side of my life to take advantage of the occasions when I could've helped you. That was wrong of me, and I'd like to put it right now. For Carey's sake, I want us to be friends.'

'Van didn't think you'd cast Ginnie yet. Is that what you're offering me?'

'Ginnie's all wrong for you, and too young for you, and I think you know it. But I'll find you something—and it'll be better for you than Ginnie. I'll find you a role with meat in it, that'll kick-start a new phase in your career. After all, I now own a film production company, don't I?'

A tear rolled down her cheek, leaving a line of watery black mascara in its wake. 'Will you really? D'you promise?'

He nodded. 'You're still a great actress, and I'll find you something worthy of your talent.'

'Thank you, Matt.' She wiped her face with the back of her hand, and then she patted her chignon and smoothed down the skirt of her dress. 'If you'll really help me, I won't be signing anything tomorrow.'

'You can be sure I will.'

'Well, then,' Cybill said, her voice shaking. 'I might as well leave now. After all, I've an appointment to cancel. I'll see you at the end of the week, Carey.'

Ignoring Leigh, she turned and left the room. A trail of musky perfume lingered in the air behind her. A few minutes later, they heard the sound of a car revving up, and then driving away. Gradually, the sound of the engine was swallowed up by the distance.

Carey yawned. 'I sure am tired. I'm gonna go back to bed. I might read my book—you're always moaning that I don't read enough. See ya later!' Waving her hand in farewell, she started to walk away.

Matt caught her by the shoulder. 'Not so fast, young lady.' He looked down at her, his expression severe. 'You're not hiding behind a novel. I think we're both entitled to an explanation.'

Carey shrugged. 'I haven't a clue what you're talking about.' Her eyes were open wide in feigned bewilderment.

'Yes, you have. I played along with you, but that doesn't mean that I approve of what you did. You're not going anywhere till you've done some talking. You put Leigh in an embarrassing position this evening and she's entitled to know why.'

Carey squirmed.

'I think Carey probably spoke without thinking,' Leigh volunteered. 'She'll have blurted out the first thing that popped into her head. Isn't that right, Carey?' She smiled at her encouragingly.

'Nope.'

'What do you mean by that!' Matt exclaimed.

Carey looked up at her father. 'Like I said. Anyone can see how much you like Leigh. You weren't pretending just now, were you? You're gonna marry her, aren't you? And I *can* be your bridesmaid, can't I?'

'I think we'll let that pass for the moment. But just before you go—if you felt so strongly that you wanted to live with me that you'd divorce your mother, to use your words, why did you refuse to visit me for so long?'

Carey went red and tugged at her hair. 'I wanted to come, but it was Mom—she was kinda funny whenever I got back home after seeing you.'

She stopped.

'How d'you mean?'

'She used to sit me down and ask me lots and lots of questions. It was like the boring ol' Spanish Inquisition we did at school.'

'What sort of questions?'

'What you'd said about any producers and directors. What you'd said about your movies. If there were any other women in the house. Sort of just what you were doing. And then she used to blame you for everything—she could be real nasty about you. In the end, it was easier to say I didn't want to see you any more, even though I did.' She looked up at her father. 'I sure missed you, Dad.'

He leaned down and hugged her.

Leigh felt a sudden stinging in her eyes as she watched them.

'So can I go and read, then? And then go and see Maria? Or maybe skip the reading bit and go straight to Maria?'

'Okay. Get changed first, though. Then you can go.' He stood aside as Carey left the room with a bounce.

They stared after her until the sound of her footsteps had died away, and then they turned to face each other.

Carey's words hung in the air between them.

Not only had Matt taken it well and not denied it, he'd actually played along with Carey, Leigh thought in embarrassment.

While it had obviously helped him out of the predicament he was in with Cybill, he must have been secretly appalled by what his daughter had said. And she was frantic with worry that he was going to feel so uncomfortable about the way that he and Carey had used her, that things might never be the same between them again.

To have everything come to an abrupt end like that—she felt like bursting into tears.

A part of her desperately wanted to believe that he'd meant every word, and that he wouldn't apologise for anything, but she was frantically trying not to let herself go down a path at the end of which lay certain misery.

Her heart lay heavy in her chest.

'What are you thinking?' he asked.

'That I ought to be checking your mail and not standing here,' she said, her words falling out in a rush. 'I want to do as much as I can before Tom gets back.'

She spun round and headed for her office.

'Marry me, Leigh,' she heard Matt call after her.

She stopped in her tracks and turned into the heat of his gaze.

Her heart started racing.

He took a step towards her. 'Marry me, Leigh. I love you and I can't live without you.'

He took another step towards her.

She thought her knees were going to give way.

Clear blue eyes looked down into her face, eyes that were filled with love.

'Carey was right about me loving you. I think I've loved you from the very first day you walked into my life and turned it upside down, but I've tried to kid myself that I didn't. I've been hurt before, and I was scared of getting hurt again. But Carey saw what I felt.'

She forced a laugh. 'Carey's got a vivid imagination; that's all. And she was desperate not to go to Italy.'

'We both know it was more than that, don't we?' He put his hand to her cheek. 'Don't we, Leigh? When Carey goes to bed tonight, she'll be dreaming about the dress she's gonna wear on our wedding day. I'd like to make that dream come true for her.'

'You're just shaken after so nearly losing her,' she stammered, 'and after learning about Van's deception. In a week or so, you'll be back to normal. Tom will be here, Carey will have gone, and I might be on a plane to England. That's the only—'

He put his finger lightly against her lips to silence her.

'Let me finish. I'm hoping you won't be going back to England, not unless we go there for our honeymoon. I was gonna ask you to marry me last night, but the kidnapping got in the way. I feel as if I've been waiting for you all my life. We belong together, you and me. I love you, Leigh, and more than anything, I want to marry you.'

He bent his head and kissed her hard.

Drawing back, he looked deep into her eyes. 'That's what Carey saw—she saw how much I loved you.'

'Do you really mean that, Matt?' she said, her voice a whisper.

'I sure do. And I'm hoping that Carey saw the same thing in you as she saw in me.'

'She did. But I can't believe you love me. I want to believe it—I love you so much that it hurts. But I can't believe it. Dreams don't really come true.'

'But they can. Put me out of my misery, Leigh. I love you with all my heart, and I don't want another minute to pass without me knowing that we'll be together for always.'

'Oh, Matt,' she breathed.

'You taught me how to slow down, how to appreciate what I've got. You're fun to be with—you're brilliant company. And you're so very beautiful. I'm at my happiest when I'm with you. The rest of my life will be empty if you're not at the heart of it. Marry me, Leigh, and I promise that whatever you dream in the future, I'll make that dream come true.'

Gazing up at him, she saw the powerful love she felt for him reflected in the depths of his eyes. An uncontrollable happiness welled up inside her, and she took a deep breath.

'Oh, yes, please. I do so love you.'

For a long moment, they stared at each other with a joy they couldn't put into words.

And then Leigh melted into his arms, and their lips met in an explosion of passion.

When they drew apart, breathless, he swung her up in his arms, and with her head against his chest, he carried her into the house to take the first steps into their future together.

ACKNOWLEDGMENTS

A huge thank you to the superb Jane Dixon-Smith for yet another outstanding cover. As always, Jane has captured to perfection the tone of the novel, and created a cover that's truly striking.

Thank you, also, to my wonderful editor, Jane Eastgate, who went through the manuscript with a fine toothcomb, spotting on the way an over-liberal application of hyphens.

Hearty thanks are due, too, to my Friend in the North, Stella, who is always the first person to whom I send my completed manuscript. Stella never fails to make honest, constructive comments, and her criticism is invaluable.

A special thank you also to all of the friends I made in my six years in California, some of whom I'm still in touch with.

One of those years was spent just outside San Francisco, where I looked after two small children, and the other five in Los Angeles, which I loved, and where I undertook a variety of jobs.

In writing Leigh's story, which is a work of fiction, I've

drawn upon memories from my very happy years in California.

As ever, my membership of the Romantic Novelists' Association, and the friendships I've made among its members, has helped to make the writing process a hugely enjoyable one, and anything but lonely.

Thank you once again to my husband, Richard, for his continued support, and for his help in the house, which gives me time in which to write.

Finally, thank you, my readers, for opening my books and walking into the fictional worlds I've created.

Or almost fictional.

ABOUT THE AUTHOR

ABOUT THE AUTHOR

Born in London, Liz Harris graduated from university with a Law degree, and then moved to California, where she led a varied life, from waitressing on Sunset Strip to working as secretary to the CEO of a large Japanese trading company.

A few years later, she returned to London and completed a degree in English, after which she taught secondary school pupils, first in Berkshire, and then in Cheshire.

In addition to the novels she's had published, she's had several short stories appear in anthologies and magazines.

Liz now lives in Oxfordshire. An active member of the Romantic Novelists' Association and the Historical Novel Society, her interests are travel, the theatre, reading and cryptic crosswords.

To find out more about Liz, visit her website at: www.lizharrisauthor.com

ALSO BY LIZ HARRIS

The Dark Horizon (The Linford Series)

Oxfordshire, 1919

The instant that Lily Brown and Robert Linford set eyes on each other, they fall in love. The instant that Robert's father, Joseph, head of the family's successful building company, sets eyes on Lily, he feels a deep distrust of her.

Convinced that his new daughter-in-law is a gold-digger, and that Robert's feelings are a youthful infatuation he'd come to regret, Joseph resolves to do whatever it takes to rid his family of Lily. And he doesn't care what that is.

As Robert and Lily are torn apart, the Linford family is told a lie that will have devastating consequences for years to come.

The Flame Within (The Linford Series)

London, 1923.

Alice Linford stands on the pavement and stares up at the large Victorian house set back from the road—the house that is to be her new home.

But it isn't *her* house. It belongs to someone else—to a Mrs Violet Osborne. A woman who was no more than a name at the end of an advertisement for a companion that had caught her eye three weeks earlier.

More precisely, it wasn't Mrs Osborne's name that had caught her eye—it was seeing that Mrs Osborne lived in Belsize Park, a short distance only from Kentish Town. Kentish Town, the place where Alice had lived when she'd been Mrs Thomas Linford.

Thomas Linford—the man she still loves, but through her own stupidity, has lost. The man for whom she's left the small

Lancashire town in which she was born to come down to London again. The man she's determined to fight for

The Lengthening Shadow (The Linford Series)

When Dorothy Linford marries former German internee, Franz Hartmann, at the end of WWI, she's cast out by her father, Joseph, patriarch of the successful Linford family.

Dorothy and Franz go to live in a village in south-west Germany, where they have a daughter and son. Throughout the early years of the marriage, which are happy ones, Dorothy is secretly in contact with her sister, Nellie, in England.

Back in England, Louisa Linford, Dorothy's cousin, is growing into an insolent teenager, forever at odds with her parents, Charles and Sarah, and with her wider family, until she faces a dramatic moment of truth.

Life in Germany in the early 1930s darkens, and to Dorothy's concern, what had initially seemed harmless, gradually assumes a threatening undertone.

Brought together by love, but endangered by acts beyond their control, Dorothy and Franz struggle to get through the changing times without being torn apart.

The Road Back

When Patricia accompanies her father, Major George Carstairs, on a trip to Ladakh, north of the Himalayas, in the early 1960s, she sees it as a chance to finally win his love. What she could never have foreseen is meeting Kalden – a local man destined by circumstances beyond his control to be a monk, but fated to be the love of her life.

Despite her father's fury, the lovers are determined to be together, but can their forbidden love survive?

A wonderful story about a passion that crosses cultures, a love that endures for a lifetime, and the hope that can only come from revisiting the past.

'A splendid love story, so beautifully told.' *Colin Dexter O.B.E. Best-selling author of the Inspector Morse novels.*

A Bargain Struck

Widower Connor Maguire advertises for a wife to raise his young daughter, Bridget, work the homestead and bear him a son.

Ellen O'Sullivan longs for a home, a husband and a family. On paper, she is everything Connor needs in a wife. However, it soon becomes clear that Ellen has not been entirely truthful.

Will Connor be able to overlook Ellen's dishonesty and keep to his side of the bargain? Or will Bridget's resentment, the attentions of the beautiful Miss Quinn, and the arrival of an unwelcome visitor, combine to prevent the couple from starting anew.

As their personal feelings blur the boundaries of their deal, they begin to wonder if a bargain struck makes a marriage worth keeping.

Set in Wyoming in 1887, a story of a man and a woman brought together through need, not love ...

The Lost Girl

What if you were trapped between two cultures?

Life is tough in 1870s Wyoming. But it's tougher still when you're a girl who looks Chinese but speaks like an American.

Orphaned as a baby and taken in by an American family, Charity Walker knows this only too well. The mounting tensions between the new Chinese immigrants and the locals in the mining town of Carter see her shunned by both communities.

When Charity's one friend, Joe, leaves town, she finds herself isolated. However, in his absence, a new friendship with the only other Chinese girl in Carter makes her feel as if she finally belongs somewhere.

But, for a lost girl like Charity, finding a place to call home was never going to be that easy ...

Evie Undercover

When libel lawyer, Tom Hadleigh acquires a perfect holiday home - a 14th century house that needs restoring, there's a slight problem. The house is located in the beautiful Umbria countryside and Tom can't speak a word of Italian.

Enter Evie Shaw, masquerading as an agency temp but in reality the newest reporter for gossip magazine Pure Dirt. Unbeknown to Tom, Italian speaking Evie has been sent by her manipulative editor to write an exposé on him. And the stakes are high – Evie's job rests on her success.

But the path for the investigative journalist is seldom smooth, and it certainly never is when the subject in hand is drop-dead gorgeous.

The Art of Deception

All is not as it seems, beneath the Italian sun ...

Jenny O'Connor can hardly believe her luck when she's hired to teach summer art classes in Italy. While the prospect of sun, sightseeing and Italian food is hard to resist, Jenny is far more interested in her soon-to-be boss, Max Castanien. She's blamed him for a family tragedy for as long as she can remember and she wants some answers.

But as the summer draws on and she spends more time with Max, she discovers that all is not necessarily what it seems, and she starts to learn first-hand that there's a fine line between love and hate.

A Western Heart

(a novella)

Wyoming, 1880

Rose McKinley and Will Hyde are childhood sweethearts and Rose has always assumed that one day they will wed. As a marriage will mean the merging of two successful ranches, their families certainly have no objections.

All except for Rose's sister, Cora. At seventeen, she is fair sick of being treated like a child who doesn't understand 'womanly feelings'. She has plenty of womanly feelings – and she has them for Will.

When the mysterious and handsome Mr Galloway comes to town and turns Rose's head, Cora sees an opportunity to get what she wants. But at Rose's cost.

www.ingramcontent.com/pod-product-compliance
Lightning Source LLC
Chambersburg PA
CBHW020814190726
48285CB00006B/2285